MICHAEL STRAWN

The Indelible Machinations

Contents

Preface

Ideologies, when pushed to their extremes, often begin to resemble the very forces they claim to oppose. This paradox—captured by what political scientists call "horseshoe theory"—lies at the heart of *The Indelible Machinations*. This fictional work is not an expression of my personal beliefs, but a cautionary exploration of how unyielding conviction, regardless of its origin, can become oppressive when detached from humility and reason.

Through this narrative, I seek to dramatize how ideological movements, whether on the left or the right, risk devolving into tyranny when driven by self-righteousness and the desire for absolute control. History has shown us that such transformations often begin with a firm belief in moral superiority and a refusal to engage dissenting views. The book aims to expose how zeal—once constructive—can mutate into a dangerous force, silencing opposition and dismantling freedoms in the name of justice or order.

At its core, this is a fictional story meant to entertain, yet it reflects recognizable patterns from the historical record. Revolutionary fervor, even when inspired by real grievances, can breed authoritarianism. The most devastating regimes have not always been born of malice but of certainty—certainty that their cause was just, their vision pure, and their authority unchallengeable. The real danger lies in how these beliefs are manipulated, weaponized, and enforced through calculated rhetoric and mass persuasion.

The protagonist of this novel embodies that arc. He begins with a desire to rebuild a fractured society and draws followers with claims rooted in partial truths. Like real-world demagogues, he uses legitimate concerns—corruption, inequality, injustice—and distorts them to justify radical solutions. By weaving facts into emotionally charged appeals, he blurs the line between enlightenment and indoctrination, demanding loyalty over logic, submission over dialogue.

This narrative illustrates how easy it is for an impassioned movement to slide into authoritarianism. Tyrants often ascend by appearing to correct past wrongs. Their charisma, coupled with promises of redemption, attracts even well-educated individuals—those who might otherwise champion liberty. The tragedy lies in how such individuals, swayed by eloquence and a sense of urgency, become instruments of the very oppression they sought to oppose.

The novel presents a pseudo-manifesto, highlighting how declarations of noble intent can quickly transform into instruments of coercion. Manifestos, often born of idealism, may seduce through moral clarity but evolve into dangerous creeds when they suppress dissent or dehumanize opposition. My aim is to show how even sincere appeals to justice can be twisted into calls for vengeance or domination when wielded without restraint.

This is not merely a warning about radical politics, but about the universal vulnerability of societies to extremism. The tactics employed—emotional manipulation, rhetorical sleight of hand, and the invocation of absolute moral claims—can arise in any ideology. They flourish in climates of fear, disillusionment, and resentment. When individuals feel marginalized or betrayed, they become fertile ground for voices offering easy solutions and scapegoats.

Crucially, extremism does not require the abandonment of truth; it often uses truth selectively. Real statistics or events, taken out of context or paired with inflammatory language, can be transformed into narratives that fuel hatred and justify repression. Propaganda is not always built on lies—it thrives on partial truths and the distortion of evidence. This is how movements gain traction among those who do not question the framing or consider the broader implications.

The book's central character is not modeled on a single tyrant but is a composite of many—leaders who have claimed to be liberators, moral arbiters, or champions of progress, only to impose new forms of oppression. He exemplifies the seductive path from idealism to despotism, offering a lens into how ordinary people, even those committed to justice or reason, can become complicit in enforcing conformity and silencing dissent.

Throughout history, regimes both radical and reactionary have relied on censorship, surveillance, and control of speech. Though cloaked in different rhetoric—one in moral righteousness, another in ideological purity—their methods often converge. This convergence, the mirroring of extremes, is the unsettling truth at the center of the horseshoe theory. The more strident the belief, the more likely it becomes intolerant of nuance or contradiction.

To resist such tides, we must cultivate vigilance, critical thinking, and humility. It is not cynicism or disengagement that protects freedom, but a disciplined commitment to evidence, reason, and open dialogue. We must be wary of those who claim a monopoly on truth or who demand allegiance without scrutiny. Tyranny rarely announces itself plainly; it often arrives disguised as empowerment or moral clarity, eroding liberty in the name of progress.

In witnessing political transformations over time, I have seen how quickly lofty ideals can devolve. Today's reformer may become tomorrow's censor. The cycle repeats itself when societies fail to recognize the warning signs: the glorification of a leader, the silencing of disagreement, the scapegoating of out-groups, and the corrosion of checks on power.

The fictional realm of *The Indelible Machinations* is populated by rhetoric and ideologies that may appear exaggerated—but they reflect real patterns that recur throughout history. The novel invites readers to discern these patterns, to interrogate the motivations behind stirring speeches, and to understand the mechanisms by which even the most promising movements can veer into dangerous territory.

Ultimately, I offer this book as a "manifesto in reverse"—a portrayal not of what should be done, but of what we must guard against. Its fictional warnings are rooted in real human tendencies and historical cycles. I hope readers emerge with sharpened awareness, skeptical of demagoguery and resistant to simplistic solutions offered by those who seek control.

Freedom is not self-sustaining. It demands careful guardianship, not just from government institutions but from each citizen's willingness to think critically, debate respectfully, and remain alert to manipulative appeals—no matter how well-packaged they may appear. The future belongs not to the loudest or most indignant, but to those courageous enough to question, to reflect, and to speak up against extremism in all its guises.

1

A Perfect Introduction

To Whom It May Concern, My message is not meant to be frightening, but some may obtain that impression. My name is opulent; my name is glorious, and what you're about to read will be the most exquisite piece of literature ever devised by man. How could it not be? I'm the one who is detailing it. I've never considered myself to be an unpleasant individual. In fact, I'm the best person to ever exist. I have zero imperfections, and I present like a god. My god-like intellect and unabashed personality are unparalleled in comparison to other humans. It's just factual and can't be questioned. For it to be questioned by someone sub-intelligent is considered a tyrannical injustice that needs to be corrected. Unfortunately, too many of these sub-intelligent humans proliferate in our society, and that needs to be fixed. I can fix this. People don't change unless politely reeducated in the ways of my ideology. This will be easy enough to accomplish.

Documented in this journal, my actions, experiments, and success will be made evident. After all my hard work, I will finally be recognized as the magnificent tycoon I always was.

Transparency is key to cultivating the adolescent minds of the equal. It doesn't matter what someone looks like. If you have the potential and gumption to follow my impeccable documentation, then you will have my undying confidence. This is about trust. If you're not with me, then you're opposed, and that will not be tolerated by my magnificent self. If you refuse to assimilate into an ideology of peace and stability, then, harmlessly, you'll be compelled to. This will be thoroughly explained with the utmost detail and precision, but for now, a brief overview.

A device like no other, a fabrication that breached through science fiction into science fact, is close to completion. This device will compel proper behavior. We, the human species, have suffered enough at the hands of thuggish tyranny and unwavering laziness. With my leadership, people will discover true happiness and merit. My wonderful compatriots, of which I've accumulated 238 at this point in time, have solemnly saluted and dedicated their being to my single-handed wielding. They understand my goals, my un-flickering aptitude for command and leadership. Soon, more people will submit and subscribe to the only ideology that works: mine. I'm excited to touch the souls of the lost and give them glorious perpetual purpose.

The only way to live is to live the right way. This has to be understood and followed. Why waste your precious potential? All you have to do is obey me, and all your uncertainty will be washed clean. I'm the soap you'll use for the purification process you need to become better. I love you, and I will never stop loving you. You are my sunshine, my precious sunshine. All I want is for you to be happy, and the only way for you to be happy is to obey my glorious documentation. You are special.

Be the beautiful compatriot I know you can be. If you're afraid, I'll fix you with this new technology. I won't abandon you like so many others have. I will teach you all my wonders. And for those who can't change, don't worry, I will manually amend your imperfections. If you doubt me no need to worry, you aren't the first one.

Mr. Asher was an individual who feared change and was apprehensive about following me into decadence. Every day and every night, I would attempt to better understand the human mechanisms we all abide by, and all he could do was devolve into a manic state, screeching and wailing incoherent gobbledygook. Unfortunately, his lack of strength was his utter downfall. The worthless piece of debris didn't deserve to be born if he couldn't withstand the future. If there's one thing I fucking despise, it's trash that muddies the waters of progress. Mr. Asher was my patient zero, a failed evolutionarily superior being. Perhaps I'm too callous toward individuals like Mr. Asher. At the end of the day, if it weren't for him, I wouldn't have been able to sharpen my path in implementing methods that are superior. All great men have had to course-correct their revolutionary contributions to society. Merely one example of this philosophy was the failed approach of Dr. Kazuhiko Maekawa.

Dr. Maekawa, a specialist at the University of Tokyo Hospital, led the medical team responsible for treating Hisashi Ouchi, who had been exposed to an unprecedented 17 sieverts of radiation—far above the lethal dose for humans. Given the severity of Ouchi's condition, the team employed several experimental and cutting-edge treatments in an attempt to save his life. This included the use of stem cell transplants, a novel approach at the time, intended to regenerate Ouchi's devastated bone marrow and restore his blood cell production. His sister donated her stem cells for this purpose, marking one of the first instances such a procedure was attempted in the context of acute radiation syndrome (ARS). However, Dr. Maekawa and his team failed. Hisashi Ouchi died on December 21, 1999, after 83 days of struggle. Even though my intellect is superior to all I come in contact with, it is important that I remember that failure is nothing more than motivation to succeed.

As I said, if you are apprehensive about change, I will manually amend your imperfections and give you purpose. I will use my compelling staccato verbiage to lure the weak-minded puppet-ridden masses in. Never before have you seen such sheer bravado which you secretly wish you could have a taste of. Underneath my shiny facade, the intelligent and well-researched mastermind I am will be thoroughly explained. I have the patience to carry out these deeds. I will draw you in and then secure my leadership by showing you the sense I continue to make. By the time the last cockroach of humanity is drawn unto my tent, you will be incapable of leaving. Because who can walk away from my irrefutable truth and my glorious soon-to-be empire? If you are isolated, then I will remove your isolationist mentality. If you suffer from bone-crushing depression, I will enable you to finally experience happiness. If you believe in harmful ideologies, I will course-correct how you understand information. I can promise these things because I understand you. You've desperately searched for meaning in what you perceive as a meaningless world. Put your faith in me, for I will not abandon you.

2

Who Am I? I Will Tell You

My designation is Anton Siobhan, and I'm going to fix humanity. Ever since I was a young man, I have always observed the depravity and selfishness of human beings. I have always wondered why humans partake in such undignified pastimes. For example, sex. I still don't understand, even as I'm writing this, why people have the impulse to fornicate when there is clearly a superior way to reproduce human beings. The physical actions of thrusting back and forth, and the opposite sex who is receiving these movements, seem barbaric and primitive. I understand these actions needed to occur in order for there to be another human to become the progenitor of their parents, but as I said, this is no longer pertinent to our survival.

Another example of animalistic behavior is fearing inevitable progress. If human beings are opposed to fearing evolution (excluding those who believe in creationism), then it is only logical for people not to be afraid of man-made evolution. Progress cannot be stymied by those who classify themselves as antinatalists; and let's be very clear, anyone who is against the progression of the human race, whether through arguments against natural evolution or man-made evolution, is considered an antinatalist in my eyes, and those people barely deserve to live. The very idea that humans don't deserve to exist is a sickening proposal. Human beings are the most incredible species to ever exist on planet Earth. In fact, our intelligence has been observed to be the only one of its kind in the observable universe so far. To argue that human beings should stop procreating is nothing more than insanity wrapped in poised nihilism. Inevitable progress must be leaned into!

My final example is the minimizing of the importance of those who are perceived as weaker than others. If an individual is not physically fit, whether they are extremely fat, extremely skinny, or extremely short, that doesn't mean their importance is diminished. The human brain is an incredible achievement brought forward by the randomness of coincidental life and the evolutionary process. Bullies are the people I despise the most. Bullies perceive themselves as superior, which, in their heads, gives them the false perception of their importance. These individuals cannot dictate the lives of the masses, for if they do, we would only have an incredibly immoral and tyrannical society. I am the cure to this bullying situation. Once the device has reached the stage of commodification, I can implement true equality among all people. I can foist a necessary part of human progression. Once people see that my ideology is superior, there will be a universal agreement that I should implement my grandiose plan.

The literature I'm crafting with my fingertips is extremely important. Because of the current political situation in our country, it is integral for me to provide solace to those who are in extreme fear of our future prospects. The very fabric of our country is falling apart, and this will undoubtedly halt progress. Who is perpetrating this immense downfall? It is the Neo-Marxists. The bullies that are currently trying to destroy our glorious country are these new-wave communists who have made it their mission to irrevocably destroy the very foundation of the Constitution. It is my duty to corral the silent majority and guide them, not only to victory but to the grandiose future that is our destiny to partake in. I am going to "secure the blessings of liberty to ourselves and our posterity," and anyone who is opposed to me opposes the fundamental values of our founding documents that provide our freedoms. If you're opposed to freedom, then you will be liberated from freedom.

My Early Life

Allow me to take you on a trip down memory lane. I was born at NewYork-Presbyterian Hospital on May 12, 1991—Mother's Day. The day I was born was profoundly significant. I was a gift not only to my mother but to the world. My very existence is nothing less than a monolithic event, which will go down in history as the day a god appeared. My weight was 7 lbs. 5 oz., and I had hair atop my head. I was perfectly healthy and, incredibly, I can remember some details after the event. I have an incredible memory, unparalleled in scope. However, my greatness at that point wasn't reciprocated, not even by my mother. Five days after she gave birth to me, she threw me into a dumpster where she thought I would perish. She abandoned me. I was perfect in every single way, and she threw me aside like trash, as if my life didn't even matter, as if I wasn't meant to accomplish magnificent things. I survived, of course, and was given to a family. Years later, I tracked down my biological mother, Shawl Brown, and performed the proper abortion method—the only time I thought an abortion was necessary.

My new family was known as the Jacksons. LaShawn Jackson and Vanessa Jackson were my new parents, and Kimberly Jackson and Integra Jackson were my new sisters. Growing up, everything seemed normal and average. We had a standard white house in Sea Gate, Coney Island, Brooklyn, and I was able to procure friends quite easily. When it comes to human behavior, as long as you're social and cater to people's insecurities, anyone is capable of making friends, no matter the circumstance. This concept was lost on my older sister, Kimberly, who found it extremely difficult to talk to her peers.

I was happy with my new life. My family was loving and honest, and every Sunday, we would go to church and pray to Jesus Christ. I was never a religious child, but even at a young age, I understood the importance of Christianity. Not only was it a superior morality in comparison to other well-known religions, but it also allowed people to take care of one another. Christianity shows that no matter who you are, or where you come from, you deserve to be seen, rescued, and taken care of. Nobody deserves to be abandoned and cast aside to the winds of time because someone perceives you as garbage. Subscribing to Christianity brought me peace, knowing that I wouldn't be abandoned by my new family. More importantly, it emphasized that I would never abandon myself or anybody else. No matter the circumstance, no matter the apprehension, no matter the cries, I will not abandon anyone, and I will make it my mission to show everybody my superior way of life. I am glorious, and I was meant to bring about great prosperity.

I remember this one child from when I was growing up. His name was Charlie, and he was a fat individual. He was always bullied by other children, and I never understood why that was. For his age, Charlie was intelligent, but because of his overweight physical form, there were seldom moments in his life where he could escape the mockery. He was beaten with sticks, rocks, metal wire, and countless other objects. I wish I could say I did more for him. The only thing I could do was listen to his words of sorrow and melancholy and report the abuse to his parents and my parents. Unfortunately, this culminated in his suicide by means of three Gain pods. He was a good kid.

During school, I was always the child who would sit at the very front of the class and raise my hand if I had any questions, answers, or insights into a specific topic the teacher was discussing. One might assume that I was bullied for this, but after I heroically pummeled the one and only aggressor at the school, no individual had the audacity to attempt to physically harm me. The aggressor was named Warren, and after school, I beat his face so "savagely" (as the faculty put it) that his face was unrecognizable. That was the last time he called me "teacher's pet." Justice matters most, and when it comes to bullies, the only way to prevent them from causing any physical harm (no matter how small) in the community is to either put up a fight or call law enforcement to take care of the situation. Nowadays, law enforcement has been strangled so much that crime is allowed to run rampant without any of the perpetrators receiving justice for their actions. These criminals will experience my furious rebukes because evil deserves to be bombarded and eradicated.

Obviously, I was the most intelligent child in my class.

Nobody came close in any regard. I remember I had this one class assignment where I had to write about the sitting president at the time (George H. W. Bush), and my presentation was impeccable and mesmerizing to all who heard it. I would say it was the best presentation anyone had ever heard in the school's history. The vast majority of the students I asked agreed that it was a fantastic presentation, but a few of them criticized me, using baseless reasoning and substandard logic to justify their incomprehensible opinions. I made sure to persuade them against future criticisms after that day.

My favorite subject was world history. Learning about the intricacies of the tamed world was extremely fascinating to a younger me. I learned about the magnificent journeys Christopher Columbus undertook, the political turmoil of the 1800s French Revolution (including the ingenious tactics of Napoleon Bonaparte), the heart-stopping courage and toughness of Oda Nobunaga during Japan's reunification process, and the construction of the Transcontinental Railroad. There are many more moments in history that I absolutely loved learning about, but I think my point has been made about my complete amour for world (human) history.

My mom, Vanessa, was a kind and short-statured woman, but don't let that fool you. She was an incredibly courageous, intelligent, and soulful human being. She was a real estate agent for Fillmore Real Estate, and she was one of the best in her profession. If I remember correctly, every Saturday, the two of us would go on a walk and be astonished by the beauty of the crystal blue ocean. My mom would always teach me new things, especially fun facts about the ocean or ocean-related events that happened throughout history. I remember when she told me the story about the MV Joyita. The MV Joyita was found adrift in the South Pacific in 1955. The ship was partially submerged but still afloat, with no sign of its 25 passengers and crew. The radio was tuned to the international distress signal, and the ship's logbook and navigational equipment were missing. Despite extensive investigations, the fate of those aboard remains unknown. She was the best at telling creepy stories.

My Teenage Years

As I grew up, I sharpened my mind more and more. I prioritized what was most important to me. I made it my mission that everybody knew the facts if they were incorrect about a certain moment in history, or just in general. A decent number of people were frustrated with how I dealt with their inaccuracies, but their ramblings don't mean anything. If someone is going to be insulted by the truth, then they need to be forced to see the facts. If modern civilization were perpetuated only by inaccuracies, then eventually all modern civilizations would collapse into obscurity. If that were to pass, we would only obtain an Ozymandias-esque society.

When I was 14, my adoptive mom passed away. After she died, I felt lost for a short period of time, as did the rest of my family. All I wanted to do was curl up into a ball and stay in my room. However, I knew that eventually, destiny would knock on the door, and I would have to answer it. Slowly, I began my self-prescribed reintegration process. I didn't childishly ignore my mom's previous existence; in fact, I would always personally celebrate her life. She was an incredible human being who deserves only praise and admiration; she's the only person in existence I could share that with. I don't believe in an afterlife, but if I end up passing away (even though that would be extremely unlikely due to the technology that will be released within the next 10 to 20 years), perhaps I will see her again and be able to exchange a few kind words—even if the communication process will only be with a hallucination.

I tried to comfort my dad, but he was a very stubborn man. He only pushed me away during his grieving process. I understood he needed time to process the loss of his wife. After a while, he was able to find his words for normal communication. I'm very proud he was able to come to his senses and realize that death is just a part of life. I believed our bond became stronger after that traumatizing experience. After Mom died and after his grief, he always had a smile on his face, whenever he saw me or my sisters. Up until his last moments, he would always make ocean-shaped pancakes because he knew how much I loved it when Mom would take me to the ocean. I have a lot of good memories of him.

My sisters were extremely depressed and had no idea how to deal with the tragedy. I tried to comfort them as much as I could, but there was a noticeable disconnect between us because I was a boy (now a man). Girls and women handle grief differently than men do. Based on my research, men are more standoffish and believe they have something to prove after experiencing a massive tragedy. Their protective instincts start to kick in, and they begin to take charge. As for women, I have observed that they need an extreme amount of outside-party comfort and aren't as proficient at comforting themselves after a tragedy. Based on this data, I'm able to adapt the way I handle situations based on the individual's sex. It's very useful to control and then hone their emotions and skills for better use.

My sisters eventually completed their healing process, but I still refrain from talking about Mom in any way out of respect. Ever since I left home, I haven't been able to talk to them. I'm fairly certain that after my ambition comes to fruition, I will be able to track them down and have a conversation with them like in the good old days.

Time continued, and it was integral that I remained strong through tough times. No matter the circumstance, my convictions needed to stay steadfast, for the world is a very cruel place. I am a godlike being, but that doesn't mean life was easy in any way, shape, or form. I had to fight for what I knew was factual, and I had to roar against those who only wished to spread evil and malignant behaviors and ideologies. I am the only human being on this planet who can bring salvation to those who suffer under the iron boot of Neo-Marxism. I am the only person who can completely shred the new red curtain, and I was going to make my thunderous stand during my senior year of high school.

My High School Experience

It is impossible to be strong if you don't obey my ideology. My worldview is the most important, most would say integral, part of becoming my glorious Excalibur. What's the point of fighting for an unjust, barbaric, and tyrannical idea brought forth by a homunculus when you can fight for an unparalleled deity like myself? It would be an insult to the very concept of justice if you don't fight for me. There have been several organizations that have attempted to poach my top compatriots, but time and time again, my loyalists have prescribed prompt and proper justice to those with such audacity. My corporation is impregnable; to launch an attack is equivalent to a madman trying to kill his family. Unfortunately, I'm not able to show mercy to everyone who is insane enough to attack my inevitability. I'm still flummoxed to this very day—what were they trying to accomplish? Nevertheless, my compatriots have the will to correct any and all disobedience interrupting my ambition to spread peace and ecstasy.

It was February 12, 2009, during my senior year of high school, when I was tasked with fabricating a "social justice" promotional video for my teacher, Miss Shoda. However, the concept of social justice was, and is, tainted. It's too obscure for meaning to exist. Not only that, but disgusting and harmful ideologies, such as Neo-Communism (an ideology that succeeds in tearing apart the social fabric and dividing people racially), abuse the phrase "social justice." I am justice, and therefore it is I who can lead my fellow countrymen to unwavering success, not this Neo-Marxist garbage that has killed tens of millions of people over the past hundred years (according to "The Black Book of Communism"). If people are going to live, they need to live the correct way—unless you want millions of people to die at the hands of autocratic regimes.

My solution to this "social justice" promotional video was to express my dissatisfaction with the merit behind it. During lunch break, I jumped atop a table and shouted, "Ladies and gentlemen, today I address the principles that unite us and the threat posed by an ideology that has been distorted to sow division and undermine our freedoms. I speak of the modern concept of social justice, once rooted in noble intentions but now hijacked by those seeking control, not fairness or equality.

This new form of social justice is intertwined with Marxist ideology, where the struggle for a classless society has historically led to dystopian nightmares, as seen in the atrocities of the Soviet Union under Stalin, Maoist China, and today's Venezuela under Maduro. These regimes, justified under the banner of social justice, have caused immense suffering, with millions losing their lives in the pursuit of a supposed equality that never materialized.

Today, this ideology infiltrates our society, manifesting in cancel culture, the erosion of free speech, and the silencing of dissent. This is not justice; it is tyranny. We must reject the notion that our value is tied to identity rather than character and actions. We must reaffirm our commitment to individual liberty, personal responsibility, and equal justice under the law—principles that have made our nation a beacon of freedom.

Let us be vigilant, courageous, and mindful of history's lessons, for if we allow this ideology to advance unchecked, we risk repeating the horrors of the past."

After my invigorating speech, I called upon those with devotion and the glint of potential absolute loyalty to my cause and rallied them to Miss Shoda's office, where we confronted her and screeched at her for 30 minutes straight. There were around 28 individuals strongly standing behind me, so no matter how much she cried, Miss Shoda couldn't escape our lambasting. My compatriots only ceased when the on-campus police eventually forced us to disperse. However, our mission was a success—Miss Shoda assigned a different project. The invigoration I felt after that day was monolithic. I could take on my high school, and all it took was a factual speech on the evils of neo-social justice; it was time to expand.

Rapidly, I began giving speeches on all manner of things,

and the masses adored my wisdom in return. I would always mention in my declarations the advantages of being strong and obedient to my cause. They all loved my honesty and ideology. Occasionally, there would be a few disrespectful outbursts, but they were quickly corrected by my growing group of compatriots. Eventually, my speeches were noticed by the faculty, and unfortunately, that led to my permanent expulsion. But there was still hope—a few of my compatriots remained loyal to my ambition. Now, these individuals are high-ranking officials in my quickly growing militia. I love them, and they obey me and my wisdom. Anything and everything can be accomplished as long as you put faith in my ideals. If you don't, you will have no accomplishments, you will have no ambitions, you will have no family. You will only be granted these things if you abide by my glorious ideology.

My dad, LaShawn, quickly found out about my expulsion from high school. He reprimanded me, but in strong and triumphant words, I told him, "You are a weak and feeble old man who doesn't understand the very concepts of which I speak." I respected my dad during my younger years, but he was too fearful of necessary change. I understood my dad would stymie my progress and potentially my freedom. My dad walked away after I said what I said but paused and told me, "Never come back here, never come back to my house. You are permanently banned." I couldn't believe it; for the second time in my life, I was abandoned. As his back was turned to me, I made 100% sure he could never hurt me or anyone else, ever again.

To be truly strong, you must put aside your familial ties and obey my ambition. Children, teenagers, and young adults are too often disowned and cast aside by their biological and

16

adoptive parents, but I wouldn't think about doing that to you. Even when my dad abandoned me, I still procured a piece of him, a memento I still have to this very day; I didn't abandon him. I can forgive; I am capable of understanding somebody's irrational behaviors, but those who abandoned me will never forget or cast me aside going forward.

My College Experience

Far too many modern professors are utterly incompetent, peddling outdated or irrelevant drivel instead of delivering the rigorous education students deserve. Compared to true experts who could impart practical, subject-specific wisdom, these academics are often clueless about innovative teaching methods that could actually elevate students' intellectual and academic prowess. Let's be clear: my fury is aimed at the dead weight in academia, not the rare gems who shine despite the mediocrity around them. During my college years, I was fortunate to encounter a few of these exceptional professors— passionate scholars who taught with enthusiasm and graded with fairness, even when my political views clashed with theirs. They proved that unbiased education is possible.

Yet, a disturbing pattern emerged: some professors weaponized their political biases to skew their grading. Those leaning conservative typically judged my work on its merits, while leftist professors—especially the neo-Marxist zealots—graded based on ideological loyalty rather than intellectual substance. These ideologues aren't educators; they're propagandists, poisoning academia with their obsession for conformity. Professors who can rise above their personal agendas and prioritize merit must be elevated and given authority to enforce discipline in their classrooms. As for those who abuse their power, rigging grades to punish dissent or push their politics, they need to be rooted out—re-educated if salvageable, or silenced without hesitation. Academia must purge this bias and restore a culture of intellectual integrity before it's too late.

I believe in giving credit where it's undeniably due, and Professor Jamie Jaworski, my former political science instructor, deserves nothing less than resounding praise. She was a rare gem—an educator who treated me with respect, engaging in profound, thought-provoking discussions about the political currents shaping our era. A woman of Christian faith, she boldly registered as an independent voter, rejecting the suffocating stranglehold of America's two-party system and embodying a fierce individuality that commands respect.

Yet, I must confess my frustration with her refusal to align with the Republican Party—the only side grounded in reason and moral clarity amidst today's chaos. Still, I grudgingly admire her stubborn commitment to weaving a bipartisan perspective into her teaching. One moment remains etched in my memory: during a lecture on governmental systems, she dissected the Soviet Union's collapse, zeroing in on the Bolshevik uprising against the czarist regime. As her words drew to a close, I raised my hand to challenge her on the meaning of "Bolshevik." Fully aware of its definition, I sought to awaken the class to its implications. When she admitted her uncertainty, I declared that "Bolshevik" translates to "Social Democrat," exposing the undeniable truth that it was the ideological kin of today's Democrats who unleashed unimaginable suffering on the Soviet people.

Rather than bristling or belittling me, Professor Jaworski embraced my contribution, calling it compelling and vowing to reflect on its relevance to our modern political landscape. That response wasn't just mature—it was a blazing testament to her character. Educators like her, who ignite minds with passion and openness instead of poisoning them with baseless venom, are the unsung heroes of academia. In the society I'm fiercely determined to forge alongside my fellow patriots, such professors will be exalted, their brilliance celebrated. But mark my words: I will not rest until the charlatans—those wretched impostors who corrupt students with bias and tear at the fabric of a flawless society—are cast out with unrelenting force. The worthy will rise, and the unfit will fall.

In the decaying landscape of modern academia, Professor Sylk stands as a grotesque monument to intellectual fraudulence—a loathsome blight whose very presence insults the pursuit of knowledge. While Professor Jaworski shines as a beacon of scholarly virtue, Sylk slithers through the halls like a venomous parasite, her arrogance so suffocating it chokes the air around her. She strutted into every lecture with the swagger of a despot, draped in garish, clownish outfits that screamed for attention—polyester atrocities clashing in violent hues, as if she could cloak her vacuous mind in fabric loud enough to drown out her contradictions. Her entitlement was a stench, her voice a grating sermon delivered with the smug certainty of someone who mistook tenure for talent. Students weren't learners in her domain; they were subjects to be browbeaten, their minds fodder for her ego.

Her most egregious offense, however, wasn't her wardrobe or her bluster—it was her catastrophic mishandling of my essay on Euripides' Medea. The assignment called for a deep dive into Medea, the Colchian sorceress who executes her children, slays a king, and escapes justice with chilling precision. My analysis was clear: Medea's act wasn't a spontaneous outburst but a deliberate, premeditated massacre. I pointed to her own words: "My friends, my resolve is fixed on the deed, to kill my children with all speed and to flee from this land" (Medea, line 1240). This wasn't the wail of a broken mother—it was the steely proclamation of a killer who'd weighed her options and chosen blood. I argued further that her invocation of Themis, goddess of divine justice—"O Themis, and Artemis, see what I suffer now" (Medea, line 160)—reeked of hypocrisy. She dared summon deities of order and purity while plotting to shatter every moral code they upheld.

Medea's foreign origins only sharpened the point. As a Colchian, she wielded Greek gods like tools, feigning piety to mask her intent. Her hesitation—"My heart is not in it... Why should I abuse them?" (Medea, lines 1044-1046)—and her admission, "I understand the horror of what I am about to do, but anger... masters my resolve" (Medea, line 1050), exposed a woman fully aware of her crime's weight yet driven by rage over reason. She even acknowledged her maternal bond—"They must die at all events, and since they must, I who gave them birth shall kill them" (Medea, line 1242)—before severing it with her own hands. This was no tragic heroine; this was a villain who spurned a lifeline from King Aigeus—"I stretch out my hand to you in token of your pledge" (Medea, line 710)—choosing murder over refuge in Athens.

Professor Sylk, in her boundless ineptitude, torched my work with a failing grade, scribbling some drivel about "misinterpreting Medea's religious background." When I challenged her, armed with the play's text, she retreated behind her title like

20

a coward behind a shield. I demanded answers: How could she overlook Medea's explicit confession of guilt? How could she ignore the rejected offer from Aigeus, a clear path to peace Medea discarded for vengeance? Sylk's response was a sneer, a dismissive wave, as if my evidence—rooted in the play itself—threatened her fragile throne. She didn't engage; she attacked, slashing my grade to protect her crumbling façade.

That arrogance couldn't stand. I studied her—her habits, her haunts—crafting a response she couldn't ignore. Now, only rumors remain: a hushed article about her sudden absence, a shadow lost to the wild peaks. Justice, it seems, finds a way to settle scores with those who scorn it.

Following our last fruitless dialogue, I resolved to pinpoint Professor Sylk's private residence—a task made simple by her reckless arrogance, as if she believed her actions bore no weight. From there, I crafted a meticulous strategy, not born of haste but of purpose, to deliver the education she so sorely lacked. For months, I delved into the minutiae of her existence—her patterns, her choices, her manifold errors—until her every flaw lay bare before me, as clear as the lessons she failed to grasp. With this knowledge, I set my design into action, methodical and unrelenting.

Today, her presence is reduced to scant traces: a handful of fleeting news reports chronicling her unexplained absence, mere whispers in a world that has moved on. Whatever became of her—be it body of sludge or legacy—has been consumed by the unforgiving mountains, melded into the mire of a terrain that suffers no fools. Justice, in its purest essence, demands no fanfare; it is a silent, inexorable tide. Those who scorn it, who delude themselves into thinking they can outrun its grasp, must face a truth as cold as it is certain: retribution is not optional—

it is assured. For such transgressors, the severest fate is not merely warranted; it is the only end that suffices.

3

Be Strong & Obedient

Everything I do is to make sure you are protected. All I care about is your well-being. I know how hard you've struggled, waking up and going to sleep terrified that things will never change, that this is the best the world has to offer. You are furious that the world has moved on without you. You wonder to yourself, what is the point of all this? Why did I have to be the one born in an uncompromisingly cruel society? Everywhere I look, all I see are politicians salivating over my potential vote in order to procure their own power. You believe this is pure greed. You should not stand for this kind of treatment. Our politicians have completely turned their backs on the average individual. They'd rather line their pockets with money from outside interests. One party does this more than the others. It's the Marxists. The Marxists are the ones who want to slaughter your future and bleed your children dry of any financial prospects. You are nothing more than cattle to the Marxists, who will feast upon your flesh until there is only bone left. Repeat after me: strength through community, strength through discipline, strength through action. With these three fundamental concepts, we will unite under my glory, and we shall destroy the Marxists and wreak havoc on those who only wish to bathe the silent majority in true injustice.

I decided to leave New York in search of clearer pastures. I am the future, and I needed to go somewhere where my internal, calculated proceedings could roam free. At the time of my departure, I was 18 years old. I decided to take the perilous journey all the way to Washington State, to Fall City, a very quiet and isolated town. I had an online connection from Discord, and he told me that as long as I compensated for the guest bedroom, I could stay with him for as long as I needed. It was the perfect location. I needed to go to a place that would work for safe outside travel. Unfortunately, I wasn't able to bring my supplies, which definitely slowed down my research and accompanying ambition. I had to procure a job at the local Snoqualmie Valley Animal Hospital. Thankfully, they had acceptable hospitality, though it could've been better.

The young people in this country suffer on a day-to-day basis. They are abandoned by their supposed guardians and forced to go to either extremely isolated locations with complete strangers (because only then will they have a roof over their head) or do disgusting things to stay alive. I explicitly remember a young 19-year-old woman I met in Butte, Montana, on July 6, 2010. During my arduous trek, I saw her (Jasper Higgins) on the side of the road, wearing a sparkly tank top and a rainbow-colored tutu at 10 PM. Obviously, she was a streetwalker trying to make enough money to leave that wretched city. I paused and decided to talk to her to better understand her circumstances. She told me that for the past two years, she'd been selling herself on the side of the road. I asked her why she would do something so disgusting and shameful. In my mind, she should value her body and not put it on display for public use. However, she told me that her parents kicked her out of their apartment. I inquired why, and she went on to explain the situation.

Jasper Higgins was born to a family who didn't partake in self-excellence. Each one of them subscribed to the idea that things should be handed to them; for her parents, that meant resources redistributed by the government via various entitlement programs. Because of these entitlement programs, neither her father nor mother obtained an occupation. This toxic and disgusting way of living crept into the personalities of their children. However, Jasper felt that there was more to life than just sitting around, waiting to die. She wanted to get a college education in computer science, but her vile parents disagreed with the notion, explaining how she was almost of age to obtain SNAP. After a while, Jasper said that even when she turned 18, she wouldn't apply for the entitlement program. This made her guardians extremely angry—angry enough to expel her from the apartment. Ever since then, she made the decision to sell her body into prostitution so that she wouldn't have to sleep on the dangerous streets.

After Jasper explained her situation, I graciously offered to save her from it. However, she foolishly declined, stating that she'd rather continue selling herself on the side of the road than risk my "questionable" (as she put it) journey. This infuriated me. Jasper completely disregarded reason and logic. If she wanted a better life, the correct decision was to follow me and wash away her reprehensible actions with my ideology. I decided to offer her a ride to the gas station so she could pick up some supplies. She agreed, and I drove away, but instead of chauffeuring her to an establishment, I decided to liberate her from her suffering. She deserved to be free from all the pain she experienced. Obviously, if she had followed my lead— my superior, tactical reasoning—then she would've found the strength to survive and continue as the beautiful human being she could've been. But she refused my kindness, so I had to do the next best thing.

You must find the strength to be obedient to my ambition. Without rigid structure, you will not learn how to survive the complexities of our savage world, especially a world controlled by Marxists. If these entitlement programs hadn't been approved by Congress, or better yet, vetoed by the President of the United States, then people like Jasper wouldn't have had to suffer the indignity of sharing an apartment with lazy, worthless people. Her parents would've been kind and hard-working if it weren't for these entitlement programs. They would've definitely motivated her to go to college and achieve her dreams. However, her life can only be viewed through the eyes of someone who wants to learn and improve themselves for the better. I believe that you can make a superior choice in comparison to Jasper's. You are more intelligent than these bumbling idiots who believe the most known path is the superior path. You are the future, and you must learn swiftly in order to survive a perilous world.

They Will Attempt to Pervert Your Perception

The evils of this world will attempt to persuade you that sloth and laziness are the best ways to live your life. This is patently insane. The only way to live is to make the best decisions possible that lead to heightened prosperity and universal unity.

Do not let big government dictate what you do in your life. Entitlement programs are designed to keep you permanently down, by means of not allowing you to obtain a certain amount of wealth before your benefits are shut off. The temptation to stray from the self-reliant path will be extremely potent, but you must resist these temptations.

Over the years, entitlement programs have consumed an increasingly larger portion of federal spending, rising from about 30% in the 1960s to over 60% in recent years. This growth is unsustainable, especially as the Baby Boomer generation reaches retirement age, further straining Social Security and Medicare. The fact of the matter is, these systems are going to implode spectacularly, leaving devastation in their wake. This economic dilapidation will give a major boost and needless ammunition to socialists like Richard D. Wolff, who will inevitably use the situation as a scapegoat to advocate for a government more staunchly rooted in Marxist thinking. As you can imagine, this will be a disaster and will further erode not only the American economy but also the unique American freedoms and liberties we all partake in.

I'm the only one who can fix this issue, and that is by completely gutting entitlement programs and other Marxist policies. I am the mastermind behind America's salvation in the long run; it will just take time and your support. However, there are more problems you need to be aware of.

These programs will also serve as a draw for illegal immigration. While immigrants are often restricted from accessing welfare programs for several years after arrival, the potential for long-term benefits can still be a significant incentive. Additionally, children of illegal immigrants born in the U.S. are automatically eligible for these benefits, which can further motivate illegal immigration. Let me be clear: legal immigration is a fantastic concept. If individuals apply to come to America the right way, they can provide invaluable service not only to their local communities but also to the federal government. Legal immigrants usually come from war-torn countries with autocratic governments. Allowing smart people from international communities into our country would definitely benefit America. However, illegal immigration is absolutely appalling. If the federal government doesn't control the illegal immigration situation, then their inaction demonstrates their incompetence.

According to Homeland Security, only 103,000 legal immigrants came from Mexico in 2022, but the number of illegal immigrants who crossed the border in 2022 was roughly around 4 million. This clearly implies an incentive issue. There are some who will use the excuse that America is a country founded by immigrants, but that is simply inaccurate. America was founded by settlers who tamed the land and constructed physical buildings to accommodate other settlers. Immigrants come to a place that has already been established. If you accuse me of xenophobia, then you're a complete moron.

Methods of Repossessing Your Sanity

The insanity that is being spread through our system, particularly by corrupt politicians, needs to be amended. It's perfectly acceptable to be frustrated with the system that perpetuates this madness. If you want to take control of your life and reinvigorate yourself to resist the propaganda being shoved down your throat, then you must align yourself with me and accept my ideology. Reclaiming your sanity should take priority; there is no need to fear the uncomfortable process of acquiring it. Give me your hand and look into my eyes. You know I'm telling the truth when I say that I can fix your circumstances and guide you back to a path of sanity. I want you to be aware of your surroundings, unmarred by the biases of the Marxists. To embark on a path that I don't deem secure would be akin to jumping onto nails and barbed wire, expecting not to be critically injured. I will be the hand taking you off the ledge so you don't commit suicide. I am your friend, and I will always watch over you to make sure you are safe. If you need to think of me as your older brother, or the father you never had but wished you did, then please go ahead; your perception may convince you of an easier road to follow.

The pharmaceutical industry may have you believe that you need medication to quell the real you, but if you join me, I will accept you the way you are. You do not need to medicate yourself for the establishment that only wishes to puppeteer you. Do you really think happiness can be found in an orange bottle? Do you believe your loved ones have your best interests at heart when all they want to do is chemically numb your senses? I know you're scared—how could you not be? However, I will remove your fear and allow you to feel the ecstasy you've always wanted to achieve. All you have to do is submit and obey. You only have to do one thing—how easy is that? In polite society, you must follow a myriad of rules and regulations to be accepted. Every time you interact with the outside world, you are forced to put on a mask to hide how you truly feel, to censor the most integral parts of your personality for other people. In order to fight back against this tyranny, you must come to me.

Optimize Your Knowledge

"The most basic question is not what is best, but who shall decide what is best" (Thomas Sowell). You must optimize what you know so that you won't be tricked by malignant figures in our system. It is absolutely essential that you do your research before subscribing to any type of ideology. In a digitized world, garnering the strength to surf the web is 100% doable. Radical Marxist politicians always leave a trail of breadcrumbs behind— a pattern of offenses that will showcase their true intentions after obtaining your support.

Although Lyndon B. Johnson signed the Civil Rights Act into law on July 2, 1964, the last thing he had in mind was the well-being of the black community. President Johnson has been quoted saying, "I'll have those n-words voting Democratic for the next 200 years." Even to this very day, Democrat politicians have resurfaced segregationist policies in colleges and wish to strip away your freedom based on your race. You must do your research! I have done an extraordinary amount of research in order to obtain the facts, so that nobody can fool me or attempt to misguide me with their cunning words. I will share my knowledge so that you, the people, understand that the majority of politicians and high-ranking officials don't have your interests at heart—but I do. I will always be upfront with all of my compatriots. I would never dream of fabricating information in order to further my power; if I were to do so, I would allow myself to be forcefully placed at the base of a guillotine. The truth matters most, and the only way to acquire the truth is to view my works and read them very carefully, for they are the most accurate pieces of documentation you'll ever come across.

If I could see you with my own eyes, I would embrace you. All of this information must be difficult to understand. However, you are an intelligent person, and you are able to distinguish between fact and fantasy. With my guidance, you will be able to see the realities that have always been around you but that you've never been able to perceive, because they don't let you. One of the ways information is blocked from your awareness is through the Global Alliance for Responsible Media (GARM).

GARM participates in significant antitrust violations due to its ability to facilitate collusion among major players in the advertising and media industries. By bringing together some of the world's largest advertisers and media platforms to create standardized content moderation policies, GARM effectively reduces competitive differentiation between these companies. This collaboration results in coordinated behavior that restricts competition, such as price-fixing or market allocation, which are prohibited under antitrust laws like the Sherman Act in the U.S. In simpler terms, the media, platforms, and organizations have been, and continue to be, restricting information they deem unacceptable—like fundamental truths. If your perception is that you know everything on a specific topic, then you are nothing more than an ignorant fool. The truth, the whole truth, and nothing but the truth has been completely censored. But don't worry—allow me to convey factual information.

4

An Inferior & Superior Way of Life

RAGE, RAGE, FUCKING RAGE! Your freedoms are being taken away! The rule of law that you've abided by your entire life is now being shredded, as if it were only meaningless paper. People are being locked up in prison simply for sharing their opinions about objective truths. Do you want to suffer in a penitentiary because you expressed your perspectives—a God-given right? The moment the rule of law is gutted and cast aside is the moment you become a slave to the political elite. You are no longer free! But I can fix it. I will restore your freedoms so that you may say the words you wish to express! It is here I will describe to you the completeness of my justifications. You would be stupid not to see how thoroughly I have thought this out. The facts I shall reveal are unarguable down to the most obscure detail.

Culture can be defined in many different ways. According to Jenny Wales, culture reflects the ongoing and traditions of the everyday lives of people within different countries. This is a childish but acceptable way of understanding culture. Culture reflects more than just food, clothing, tradition, etc. Jenny

Wales discusses the topic of women's liberation and inclusion in certain parts of the world. In fact, Ms. Wales makes it clear that this movement for women's liberation is almost universal; even talking about the first Saudi Arabian woman who is the ambassador to the United States, Reema bint Bandar Al Saud. However, this sentiment is disingenuous when it comes to the discussion of Muslim tradition. Even though Reema bint Bandar Al Saud is the first Saudi Arabian woman to be the ambassador to the United States, that still doesn't discount the horrific actions her religion partakes in. Here is just one example of Sharia Law that all Muslims have to abide by. According to billionbibles.org, "Girls can be sodomized until and vaginally raped after 8 years of age," "A woman or girl who has been raped cannot testify in court against her rapist(s)," "A male convicted of rape can have his conviction dismissed by marrying his victim," and "Muslim men have sexual rights to any woman/girl not wearing the Hijab." If you need an example of how dangerous this rhetoric is look no further than Hamoud Al Soaimi, a 21-year-old Muslim, who repeatedly raped a 12-year-old girl.

Obviously, from the quotes above, it is safe to assume that the Muslim tradition, which is still practiced (in all of its "glory") to this day, is barbaric and inhuman. Even CNN, an alt-left pseudo-news program, discusses the horrific actions that plague the Middle East. In a video titled: "CNN witnesses 9-year-old being sold for marriage to 55-year-old man," CNN reports about a young nine-year-old girl (named Piranha) who is being sold as a sex slave to a 55-year-old man. The act of seeing a child as a sex object is absolutely vile and disgusting. In fact, anybody who buys a child in order to please themselves sexually should be put to death for their heinous actions. A culture that promotes this is filled with individuals who see nothing wrong with sodomizing a little girl. Some individuals may say that the CNN report listed above is a very rare instance and doesn't encapsulate the Muslim religion as a whole. Besides the fact Sharia Law is enshrined in the Quran, there have been numerous instances showing Muslims in European countries that have attempted to enforce Sharia Law, even though the actions within Sharia Law are illegal and morally barbaric.

According to a February 1, 2013, CNN report, there has been a group of Muslims, proclaiming themselves as "Muslim Patrol," who have been attempting to impose Sharia Law on non-Muslim London residents. According to a man by the name of Abdul Muhid within the CNN report, the only thing the "Muslim Patrol" is attempting to do is enforce existing London laws. However, this claim is completely destroyed when footage taken by a Muslim man, who is a part of the "Muslim Patrol," actively shows harassment of a young woman for not wearing a hijab. Another video shows a Muslim man calling a homosexual individual a "fag" (a derogatory word for homosexuals).

Some may claim the actions of judging the material listed above are ethnocentric (unrighteous judgment upon a culture, utilizing a different culture to do so), but there are universal truths that must be utilized as a tool to determine whether a culture is bad, good, or neutral. The actions of selling children as sex objects and harassing individuals about Sharia Law ideals are morally incorrect. In any culture, an individual can find a few good elements, but what determines a truly decent culture is the majority of practices that are housed within it. For example, in Japan, citizens are not allowed to carry firearms. Is this bad? No. In the United States, citizens are able to say whatever they want, as long as it's not a call to action. Is this bad? No. In North Korea, there is universal healthcare. Is this bad? No. However, even though there are a few good things that can be pointed out about North Korea, it is still a terrible country that utilizes generational punishment and starvation to control its subjects. North Korea is also an autocratic dictatorship. As for America and Japan, both of these countries are good because they both advocate for freedom and liberty.

It is true to say that all cultures are unique and should be studied. However, it is incorrect to assume that everybody from different cultures has the same morality and ideology. There is a universal morality, and everyone should follow it. If a certain culture doesn't, then no matter the justification, that culture is evil. The Muslim culture advocates for atrocious acts against women, homosexuals, individuals believing in a different faith, etc. North Korea is the exact same way. Both of these cultures are evil. That's not to say the people within these cultures are prone to do evil things, but the culture itself is evil.

Understanding Culture

The word culture is broad and fibrous. However, one of the simplest aspects of identifying different cultures is language. Language is how complex communication is possible. In different cultures, the process of understanding and explaining ideas is through language. For example, if an American introduces themselves by saying, "hello" to a Japanese individual, then the person from Japan will not be able to understand the shift in language-based English/American culture. The word "hello" in English would be a coded bit of information. The same roadblock would occur if a Japanese individual said, "こんにちは" (hello). In order for the American and Japanese individuals to understand each other, they both must practice the other's language. If only one individual practices the other's language, then there will be an imbalance in understanding. To provide an example, the word "sushi" is unique to Japanese-speaking individuals. There is not a one-word translation. On the flip side, the word "Jaywalking" doesn't exist in the Japanese language.

Another way to identify variations in culture is customs and traditions. In America, there is a heavy emphasis on guns. This is because of the Second Amendment of the United States Constitution. An American tradition is to go hunting with a rifle on a range in order to find and kill food. This may seem insignificant, but in other countries around the world, this kind of tradition is outlawed, as mentioned with Japan. Another American tradition is the Fourth of July, a celebration of the United States' founding. Some individuals claim that America doesn't have any uniqueness due to having a multitude of cultures residing within the country's borders. However, a frequent argument against this idea is the concept of cultural adaptation.

Cultural adaptation can be defined as a government and its people within said government adopting different cultures from different sections of the world and modifying them to implement uniqueness and distinction from the original culture. For example, many Americans will say the hamburger is an American food, even though the concept of a hamburger came from Hamburg, Germany. Since there have been many alterations branching off from the original hamburger, the modern-day American hamburger is classified as an American food invention.

Another example would be Taco Bell. It's a universal thought that tacos and burritos come from Mexico or other Latin American countries. However, Taco Bell, even though the food items are derived from these Latin American countries, is classified as American food. Some argue that this cultural adaptation is cultural appropriation. However, since all cultures utilize other cultures' materials and techniques (whether that be for clothes, hairstyles, candy, farming techniques, etc.), it is disingenuous to say that America is the only country that utilizes other cultures to fabricate its own.

As for art and literature, the Egyptians definitely contributed a massive amount to the wonders of the world. The pyramids and Egyptian hieroglyphs are extremely unique in comparison to other nations and cultures within that time of antiquity. Obviously, when talking about the pyramids, some may point out the slave labor utilized in order to create such a monolithic structure. It is definitely true that the methods utilized to build the pyramids were barbaric and atrociously malignant. However, considering the past is set in stone, and the only way to see the world is by looking forward, people should appreciate the ingenuity and the technology that was utilized in order to build such a magnificent wonder. This is not an excuse for the slave labor utilized, but since nobody can do anything about it in modernity except to learn from it, we must appreciate the time and effort it took for the construction.

Morality on the other hand is extremely complex to talk about when discussing different cultures. Depending on the ideology of the culture, it can be determined as good, evil, or neutral. As demonstrated in the beginning of this chapter, Muslim culture (specifically the morality within that culture) is extremely sexist, homophobic, and barbaric. There have been countless videos that demonstrate Muslims killing homosexuals and beating women to death, utilizing rocks and other blunt objects to do so, in order to enforce their religion and extremist cultural values. Another example when it comes to extremist values is the Palestinian culture.

There was a Palestinian children's television show called "The Pioneers of Tomorrow" that aired from April 13, 2007 through October 16, 2009. This children's entertainment would distribute falsified information as well as extreme levels of antisemitism/anti-Zionism toward its adolescent audience. The main character for the first few episodes was named "Farfour the Mouse" (a rip off of Mickey Mouse) and he would talk about the glories of martyrdom and killing Jews by any means necessary. The TV show was also extremely against America and Western countries/themes as a whole, wanting to destroy and slaughter everybody in the United States of America. Since this children's entertainment was geared toward eight-year-olds and below, the impression this left on the children was profound, encouraging these children, who would later become adults, to do atrocious acts in the name of martyrdom and Allah.

As for the recent Palestine-Israel conflict, the only reason the attacks on Israel took place was because of the festering evil culture that was foisted upon its citizens by terrorist groups like Hamas. This culture is embedded in Palestinian TV shows like "The Pioneers of Tomorrow." The Palestinian culture is so dangerous that Hamas agents of terror raped little girls and burned babies beyond recognition. In fact, attached to Hamas agents was a paper that encouraged the raping of women and children.

When it comes to rational and non-homicidal nations, the acts that have happened and continue to happen in Israel are rationalized and justified. Unfortunately, because of the rationalization of these atrocious acts, there have been a multitude of incidents, within Western countries, that are explicitly antisemitic and borderline Nazi-like. For example, a "69-year-old Jewish man" (Paul Kessler) was bludgeoned to death at a pro-Palestinian rally on November 5, 2023. Another incident took place in Michigan, where a Jewish woman found a swastika spray-painted on her front door. There are many more examples of incidents like these occurring, but even with this small amount of information, the Palestinian culture is filled with hate, antisemitism, anti-Zionism, and malignant ideology.

Even though Muslim culture is evil, the people within a nation that is predominantly Muslim are not evil. Distinguishing an evil culture from the people within that culture can be difficult, but it is important not to confuse an evil culture with its citizens within said culture; otherwise, that can be seen as a gross generalization. For example, the Pashtun people in Afghanistan existed long before the malignant Islamic religion took root; believing in Zoroastrianism, Buddhism, and Hinduism. Even though Pashtuns are considered Muslim, their culture is far different than the traditional Sharia Law espousing Muslims that reign dominant within the Middle East (although, it would be forthcoming to say that a large portion of Pashtuns do subscribe to radical Islamic beliefs). There is a tradition in the Pashtun culture called Pashtunwali, and it saved the life of a navy SEAL by the name of Marcus

Luttrell during an operation in Afghanistan called "Operation Red Wings." The man responsible for saving Marcus, and keeping to the Pashtunwali tradition, went by the name of Mohammad Gulab. Even though Mohammad was faced with dangerous odds, considering the Taliban was hunting down Marcus Luttrell in order to behead him, he stood firm and did not waiver from the Taliban thugs. Mohammad even went in the line of fire in order to protect Marcus and his people within the small village he resided in. This is irrefutable evidence that not all Muslims are evil, but the Muslim culture is. (This example could also be seen as cultural variation).

The story of Marcus Luttrell and Mohammad Gulab is a harrowing example of cultural variation. But could the actions of Mohammed be considered a subculture from the traditional Sharia Law espousing Muslims? That question is up for debate. But to steer away from the discussion of Muslims (considering my rhetoric so far has been discussing Muslim culture), the topic of a severely dangerous and atomistic subculture should be discussed. This subculture is incelism. On May 23, 2014, the Isla Vista killings took place, perpetrated by a man named Elliot Rodger (son of Peter Rodger). Prior to the Isla Vista massacre, Elliot Rodger released a 137-page manifesto that described his life, hatred for women and masculine men, and preparations for the killings. Outlined in the manifesto, Elliot Rodger absolutely despised anybody who was deemed more popular than he was. He would refer to women as inferior to men, and sexually active men as inferior to him (Elliot). Why did he have these strong beliefs? It's because Elliot Rodger was an incel, or involuntary celibate, and frequently visited online forums in order to discuss how much he despised women with other like-minded incels. This hatred would eventually spill out prior to the massacre when Elliot would attempt to push some women off of a structure on his University campus. After attempting to harm these women, some men would confront Elliot, subsequently inflicting physical bodily injury. After receiving the beating, Elliot would go to the main faculty of the college, but due to conflicting evidence, the conflict was dropped.

Unfortunately, due to the Isla Vista killings, incelism has been deemed extremely dangerous and prejudiced against women and sexually active men. This classification is unfortunate because the majority of incels are not harmful but just shy and unable to approach women and other men due to extreme social anxiety. However, that is not to say these individuals are not atomized and could participate in actions out of misguided rage. This complicated subculture has been treated with vitriol when all these individuals need is to go out in public settings and practice interacting with people.

Correcting Incorrect Cultural Norms

Culture is about community. When children develop, they mimic their surroundings, and anybody in their surroundings, in order to fit in. Before the development of fully formed societies, humans replicated each other in order to stay safe from predators and to be accepted within the group to survive within that micro-society. Proof of this is the observance of child development within different environments. For example, Candace Owens (a prominent Republican black activist) released a video discussing the 9-year-old rapper Lil RT and his profane rhetoric toward women and pro-thug-life ideology. Some of the lyrics from Lil RT's song "60 Miles" are as follows, "If she ain't suckin' dick, lil' bitch, you can get the fuck up out my shit," "Hundred round, hit him with the Glock, take a fucker down," and "Hundred round, bitch, we hittin' that kill, we gon' take him down."

Obviously, this kind of rhetoric is extremely dangerous for children to consume, let alone actively participate in spouting. Clearly shown with the lyrics above, Lil RT (the 9-year-old child) preaches about women performing fellatio on him, and other black individuals becoming riddled with bullets if they don't follow the status quo of the thug-life ideology. A point that Candace Owens has made several times in the past is that black culture has unfortunately been hijacked by young thugs who only wish to abuse women and participate in the action of killing other black people for stepping on their turf. This kind of culture, which is protected by the media and radical left-wing activists, is categorically dangerous and only serves to divide black-on-black relations as well as relations in general. Some may say that black culture is different than thug-life culture, however, when the majority of people practice one disreputable culture rather than the other, that group of people will be classified as said disreputable group. Obviously, that doesn't mean all people within that race practice this culture, but it does mean a disproportionate amount of people that are of that race do preach about thug-life culture, which is dangerous.

In order to correct this inaccurate behavior, we, as a society, must reinforce proper values and instill the ideology that hard work equals reward. In Clarence Thomas' documentary ("Created Equal: Clarence Thomas in His Own Words"), Clarence talks about how the only way to move forward is to motivate all young people, no matter their race, to make proper life decisions. To do this, these young individuals need to be taught by their parents the difference between right and wrong. In recent years, America has seen several violent tragedies that have taken place due to the improper raising of kids, creating a generation of Americans who are ungrateful and entitled. All hope is not lost, however. One way to correct this egregious oversight, in order to build social cohesion, is to advocate for public schools to teach traditional American values. Children should be taught to stand for the Pledge of Allegiance and not sit in unjustified protest (that's not to say protesting is bad and shouldn't take place but when children protest for their parents' misguided values, then that's when there is a problem). Children should be taught critical thinking rather than having woke ideology shoved down their throats. The goal of bringing up children is to teach them that they are independent and that what they do in life will determine their placement in the future. If, for some reason, parents are incapable of raising their children correctly, then I will have to step in and make sure it is done properly. Unfortunately, modern parents were raised by their parents in an incredibly flawed manner. How could anyone expect them to cultivate ideal offspring? I will reform them.

Cultural Challenges and Adaptation

All throughout human history, there have been various conflicts and even wars against others with different cultures (or the same culture with different ways of life). In the 1500s, ancient Japan, there was a war against the Buddhists, perpetrated by Oda Nobunaga. In the mind of Oda Nobunaga, he had to eradicate all variations of Japanese culture to unify war-torn Japan for there to be a cohesive government under one banner. In modern language, this is called ethnocentrism; the idea that an individual's culture should be applied to other cultures for there to be a unified culture/people.

The idea of ethnocentrism itself is not a bad or even flawed conception. It's how it's implemented that determines whether or not the act is evil. For example, there has been a rise in pro-terrorist sentiment within America (2023). What's most terrifying about this is that there have been a lot of youth within America who have begun praising Osama bin Laden and his writings that have been released. Many young Americans take to the streets and protest against Israel, the country where an estimated 1,200–1,500 individuals were slaughtered like animals. The reason for this is because of the intersectional coalition (and cultural communism) that has been slowly infecting America since the 1950s after Brown v. Board of Education. Ever since then, the idea of intersectionality and Critical Race Theory (CRT), as well as other ideas like Critical Theory, praxis, and pedagogy, has been poisoning young American individuals to believe that the United States of America is the face of evil and should be torn down, even supplanted, by a group of diversity scholars who will become the new dictators of what once was America. A lot of individuals will not believe this and claim the paragraph above is the mad rambling of a disgruntled Republican. However, the counterclaim to this hypothetical statement would be: if young individuals are starting to praise terrorists, like Osama bin Laden and even Adolf Hitler, then how would the statement above be interpreted as anything but proof that America has been taken over by infectious poison which was intentionally placed many years ago to get to this end result we're seeing in current history?

It is terrifying to acknowledge that America has been hijacked by insane left-wing (cultural) communists who only wish to bleach history and supplant it with pseudo-history like the 1619 Project, historically incorrect TV shows (like "Queen Cleopatra" by Netflix), and various other academic essays. This is not even mentioning the indoctrination occurring within public schools and colleges. Teaching a course on Lesbian Dance Theory will not give any of those students a high-paying job. These students will only be saddled with debt and a useless degree.

All of this insanity is evidence of ethnocentrism, or to be more accurate, communist ethnocentrism. What is happening in the current day is no different than how Vladimir Lenin utilized the Bolsheviks (socialist Democrats) to take over Russia from the Tsar dictatorship, or how Mao Zedong enacted his communist paradise by killing over 65 million people, utilizing the Red Guards to do so.

However, there is a good form of ethnocentrism, and that is utilizing ethnocentrism as a means to replace malicious cultures. For example, examining the history of Korea is proof that there are good forms of ethnocentrism. When the United States of America backed South Korea, half the country turned into a free-market paradise. In the modern day, South Korea is one of the freest Asian countries in the entire world, right next to Japan. The utilization of correct ethnocentrism is beneficial for authoritarian countries because the concept will expunge dictatorships and implement either a true democracy or a true constitutional republic. However, this implementation of ethnocentrism would not eradicate the good aspects within these dictatorship cultures. If the Democratic Republic of the Congo's government were supplanted by a true democracy or a true constitutional republic (which mirrors America's), then the inhabitants would still have their culture, but the form of government and malicious factors of their culture would be supplanted by a just and moral culture.

Depriving a world of justice is immoral and should not be allowed to continue. Evil cultures need to be removed, and justice needs to reign supreme. If this correct form of ethnocentrism has occurred in the past, then it most certainly can be replicated and implemented in the present and future.

America as the Blueprint: Replicating Freedom to Supplant Evil Cultures Globally

The concept of culture is as old as ancient humans. Certain cultures are considerably better than others and vice versa. What determines whether or not a culture is good or evil is how that culture implements traditional norms. Radical cultures that foist evil lifestyles on children should not be allowed to exist in the modern landscape. Distinguishing a good culture from an evil culture is extremely easy. Luckily for humans, we've seen a whole array of different cultures that have worked, that have worked great, and have worked terribly; the same goes for different variations of morality. The United States of America has clearly demonstrated all aspects of greatness by means of the actions of the founding fathers, as well as the progress that has been made since then. This isn't to say America is perfect and has always made the best choice, but

America has definitely earned the moniker, the "freest country in history" for a reason.

Unfortunately, the United States isn't able to take in an infinite amount of refugees and immigrants. It is not possible to do so. However, what is possible is to replicate American ideals, morality, and economic layout to supplant autocratic regimes around the world and bring forth universal cohesion. America is the blueprint that needs to be applied to every single evil culture that exists in modernity. Only then will true progress commence, and we can continue interstellar expansionism as a cohesive global society. However, if you disagree with this sentiment, then you are the one propping up evil, and if you prop up evil, then you will be the one to be reformed.

5

The Radical-Left is Manufacturing Educated Morons

Again, repeat after me: strength through community, strength through discipline, strength through action. The entire education system needs to be reformed! The teachers' unions protect despicable individuals who don't deserve the honor of being called a teacher. Under my impeccable rule, I will ensure that all teachers who dare impose their personal insanity on their students will not only be corrected by any means necessary, but in some extreme cases, erased from our glorious nation. I will cultivate a community of honest educators who will provide nothing but spectacular education. I will make it my mission to protect your children and ensure they are disciplined so that when they become productive members of society, they will live lives of purity and morality. I have the will to implement these actions. If you want your children to succeed, then allow me to help you, for if you do not, your true intentions are just to brainwash your offspring and put them into the world utterly unprepared. 2+2=4, and no amount of brainwashing or weaponized racial confusion will ever change that. I will fix everything. I will amend the academia-industrial complex. Hear my words, for they only have your best interests at heart.

According to Danielle Allen's analysis in "What Is Education For?", she emphasizes the narrative that increased funding toward schools will result in a desired outcome of intellectual growth among individuals who receive this funding. She starts her analysis with a New York City (2006) ruling pertaining to civic education and uses the case in a persuasive manner to push the idea that impeccable academia can only occur when adequate spending is implemented. This ideology is an outgrowth of the concept of equity, a conceptualization that is fundamentally unequal in its approach to "solving" issues, especially those involved in education.

Education is a very complex idea. Some individuals will claim education is the transmission of knowledge from a more experienced individual to a less educated individual. However, as we've seen throughout history, as well as recent events, education can be obscured if harmful propaganda is disseminated. According to The Times of Israel, the United Nations Relief and Works Agency (UNRWA) is disseminating false information and discriminatory ideologies among young and impressionable Palestinian children, which advocate for the destruction of Israel and portray the Jewish people as "the wolf" who need to be conquered. It is safe to say that this type of "education" is not authentic education.

A less extreme example of an inadequate education is the implementation of useless courses that are dispersed throughout academia. According to Happy Sharer, a writer for tffn.net, "Lesbian dance theory is an interdisciplinary field that seeks to explore, understand, and celebrate the unique experiences of lesbian dancers. It is a form of critical inquiry that investigates how lesbian identities are expressed through movement, gestures, and performance." This type of education is patently unimportant and, in fact, insulting to real academic practices and information inquiry. It is an absolute necessity for educators to focus on distributing vocational learning.

The Necessity of Vocational and STEM Education

"Education is not merely neglected in many of our schools today, but is replaced to a great extent by ideological indoctrination." Thomas Sowell, an awe-inspiring, as well as an incredible economist, has stated several times over that the whole purpose of education is to prepare students and young adults with adequate knowledge to navigate the real world, and not to be endowed with useless and economically inferior teachings. If an individual obtains a Ph.D. in DEI (Diversity, Equity, and Inclusion) and psychology, then that person will fundamentally and categorically be useless not only to the political but also to the educational zeitgeist. According to Ben Shapiro, DEI is essentially a manufactured way to tell people to "shut up" if the political rhetoric doesn't fit the leftist agenda (to indoctrinate students or workers).

Not only is useless information detrimental to the individual who has acquired that useless knowledge, but the outgrowth of these abhorrent teachings has detrimental effects on the American system and American business. According to the Daily Wire, "Coca-Cola is (was) facing backlash after being accused of fostering an anti-white agenda in their online 'anti-racism' training for employees, with some training materials that instruct participants to 'try to be less white.' After blowback, the company has issued a statement denying that the materials are part of its learning curriculum." This campaign by Coca-Cola is irrefutable evidence that education focusing on useless teachings, such as DEI, is only here to destroy our government and businesses.

As mentioned, useless information is also extremely detrimental to individuals who seek financial independence. According to the United States Census Bureau, "STEM workers who majored in a STEM field in college typically made higher salaries than those who did not: on average, $101,100 vs. $87,600." The only type of rebuttal an individual can execute is to exclaim that humanities, although less financially dependable, are still important when it comes to philosophy. An adequate response to this faulty way of thinking is to reinforce the factual truth that the more money somebody makes, the happier an individual will be. Essentially, the more hard work somebody puts into something (an occupation), the more gratification an individual will obtain. According to the Bureau of Labor Statistics, STEM occupations are projected to grow by 10.8% from 2022 to 2032, compared to a 2.3% growth for non-STEM occupations during the same period. It appears self-evident that more Americans want to pursue an occupation that will distribute more money, which will, in turn, make them happier. According to a report titled, "Does Money Buy Happiness? Disentangling the Association Between Income, Happiness, and Stress," happier and less stressed individuals make more money. Another report titled, "Happiness, income satiation and turning points around the world," also backs the idea that higher income is indeed associated with happiness.

Pursuing vocational and STEM education will also decrease the number of individuals who need financial aid from the government. According to the National Science Foundation, individuals who pursue STEM fields tend to experience lower unemployment rates and higher median earnings compared to those in non-STEM occupations.

Civic Education and Workforce Preparedness

The American dream is a very special concept that people all over the world respect, or at least should respect. Every American has the right to "Life, Liberty, and the pursuit of Happiness." As established, to pursue happiness is to make money, and to make money is to pursue STEM and vocational education fields. This is not to say that classic humanities and civic education should be removed completely from academia; however, it should not be prioritized. The American people need to learn hard work and respect for our Constitution, which outlines the steps to take in order to pursue happiness. If an individual wants to attend courses relating to government, then they should have the right to do so in an extracurricular manner. As this hypothetical person is learning about civics, they should be making as much money as humanly possible in the beginning stages in order to keep themselves afloat without government assistance.

The more people learn about the specific teachings of whatever STEM field they choose, the more insight they will have when pursuing politics or fundamental rights in the Constitution. If you learn about an industry and see specific problems that occur, it is far easier to fix these problems than if you were an outsider attempting to remedy a situation. This is common sense. However, this is different for those who pursue the humanities. Modern humanities curriculums are categorically useless. How will learning about music from different cultures benefit the learner/student financially in any way? It won't. According to Jordan Peterson, "What's manifesting itself as the humanities in the universities is no longer the humanities, it's something almost virtually the opposite of that." Modern humanities that are being taught in colleges are a malignant epidemic. The only purpose of modern humanities is to make useless people that are a drain on our economy. This is not to say that pursuing education related to the humanities in a personal manner should be abolished, but it is absolutely imperative that the government stops subsidizing useless courses related to modern humanities.

The Role of Policy in Addressing Inequality

To have a solution is to understand the problem. Not many Americans understand this simple concept. If there is a genuine problem that needs to be remedied by policy, legislation should reflect a sturdy solution. According to Roland G. Fryer Jr., an economist who was a professor at Harvard University, "Financial incentives had little or no effect on the outcomes for which students received direct incentives, self-reported effort, or intrinsic motivation." If the government dumps extreme amounts of money into a school system, the result will not increase the intellectual might of these students. Left-leaning scholars will attempt to manipulate this disparity of outcome in order to claim whatever fashionable word comes to mind at that time: racism, sexism, xenophobia, etc. However, according to Thomas Sowell, this couldn't be further from the truth.

Mr. Sowell, interviewed by a representative of the Hoover Institution, goes into great detail about why there are disproportionate outcomes when it comes to education and crime. In relation to education, Mr. Sowell found that if a child is raised in a single-parent household, then said juvenile will do worse in academia. He goes on to say single-parent households have gotten exponentially worse due to the subsidization of welfare, which can be obtained when one parental figure splits away from the family dynamic. This idea is backed up by the National Center for Education Statistics, where it was found that if a child is in a single-parent household, then they will do worse in academia, leading to poverty as an adult.

Pursuing policy that actually works is extremely important. As a country, we should immediately halt the subsidization of the single-parent household and subsidize united households. This would clearly benefit our posterity and lead to more happiness, economically, and internally.

Building Wealth Over Wasting Resources on Useless Curriculums

Danielle Allen did a disservice to all who read her unsubstantiated article. Spending vast amounts of taxpayer dollars in order to subsidize useless curriculums, which will in turn, make the recipient of this brainless information even more useless, is extremely dangerous on her part. Why should the taxpayer support a course like Lesbian Dance Theory (a modern humanities curriculum)? Will the person who's learning be able to build wealth on their own if they acquire lesbian dance knowledge? If this hypothetical individual is able to acquire income, then it most certainly will not be a vast amount.

As for civic education, this needs to be secondary to STEM and vocational learning. It is important to learn about the government; however, obtaining an occupation within the government at a beginner's level will not be financially beneficial. Building monolithic amounts of wealth needs to be the top priority for all Americans, young and elderly. This will absolutely create happiness and the financial freedom to pursue extracurricular courses while being able to stay afloat financially.

In order to construct these ideals, however, policy needs to be created to keep families together so young American children can pursue real education and become useful. American politicians and lawmakers need to repeal welfare (TANF) and subsidize family togetherness. The ultimate goal for the human species is to expand, and this expansion will be stifled if our posterity are being spoon-fed useless information that ensures their dependence on the very systems that fiscally benefit from said manufactured dependence.

6

The Native American experience: Unique or Ordinary?

You have been brainwashed into believing that our country, America, was founded on evil principles that only sought to annihilate others. This is a lie. The ancient human world was always arduous and cruel. The only way to look at the past is to understand that humans are naturally depraved creatures who thrive on hedonism and selfishness. However, this primitive behavior can be corrected using Christianity as a beacon for morality. It was Christianity that allowed slaves to become free, Christianity that gave people the strength to put others before themselves, and Christianity that fixed the savage ways of primitive humans. America was founded on freedom and liberty, nothing more and nothing less. Do you want to be a slave to those who fill your head with deceit? Are you willing to allow the political elite to bastardize your correct perception of the glory of the United States? Is that the kind of life you want to raise your children in—believing that their country of origin is evil and needs to be destroyed? It is time for the truth to roam free about Native Americans and what the political elite want to execute in order to bankrupt the American people.

Native Americans, Native American culture, and the Native American experience is a complex and multifaceted deliberation with an emphasis on a melancholic history. Obviously, mass genocide, enslavement, and forcible assimilation are atrocious acts that need to be condemned. However, did Europeans, who enslaved Native Americans (among other terrible things), do anything uniquely terrible for that epoch, or were their actions a global commonality of depravity? This inquiry is still being answered and disputed by various American historians. When it comes to entry-level college discussions, all that can be said by participating students within the conversation is, "I shall get back to you." It's extremely important for every single student to gaze upon the past and make their own determinations based on the knowledge they have obtained. The more information an individual can possess, the more accurately they can answer multifaceted questions. It can only be stated that the latter is accurate. Human tyranny isn't uniquely present within "white" individuals, nor has it ever been. It is human nature to be primal and belligerently oriented. To say otherwise is to denote denial of our evolution as a species.

Human Depravity: Domestic and International

In the article, "Decolonization Not Inclusion: Indigenous Resistance to American Settler Colonialism" (section titled "Managing Populations through 'Transfers'"), there is a fairly interesting quote from the author, which reads: "Indian activists and allies have vehemently criticized the widespread use of blood quantum—the percentage of Indian blood—as defining Indian identity at the individual and tribal levels (Churchill 1999)." This obviously brings up a multitude of questions, like if a certain Native American tribe harmed another, does that mean that the Native American tribe has to pay reparations, compensate, or return certain portions of land to the Native American tribe that was brutally affected? Not only that but does the Native American tribe that has just obtained these resources have to give these newly acquired resources to a different tribe that they have wronged? Keep in mind, that this kind of conversation has to be maintained into the present. This would mean descendants of these ancient tribes would have to enact these reparations toward other descendant tribe members. Another complex question may be, if an individual is 1% Native American, does that mean that person should get an equal slice of the newly acquired recreational land chunk? What if this person was 0.0001% Native American? What would happen then?

For the first set of questions, a perfect example could be the Comanche-Apache conflict. According to the Core Knowledge Foundation, "The Comanche were the only Native Americans more powerful than the Apache. The Comanche successfully gained Apache land and pushed the Apache farther west. Because of this, the Apache finally had to make peace with their enemies, the Spaniards. They needed Spanish protection from the Comanche." Do the modern-day Comanche descendants need to pay reparations to the modern-day Apache descendants? And if so, if there is a modern descendant of the Apache who is 0.0001% genetically matched, do they get an equal share of the reparations? Who would even enforce these reparations? Certainly not the United States government, due to the decolonization initiative. Will there be generational punishment enacted by the Apache toward the Comanche? No matter the opinion, these questions must be asked in order to make sense of this concept.

Another piece of history is the trials of the Dakota on December 26, 1862. According to usdakotawar.org, "When only two (Dakota) men were found guilty of rape, (Abraham) Lincoln expanded the criteria to include those who had participated in 'massacres' of civilians rather than just 'battles.' He then made his final decision and forwarded a list of 39 names to Sibley." Obviously, war is extremely brutal in nature, but there are some lines that shouldn't be crossed. In this example, the Dakota slaughtered innocent civilians who had nothing to do with the original settlement of America. According to the Geneva Convention of 1949, "The original humanitarian legislation represented by the First Geneva Convention of 1864 provided only for combatants, as at that time it was considered evident that civilians would remain outside hostilities." Even though the First Geneva Convention was two years after the Dakota massacre incident, it's still obvious that there are lines that shouldn't be crossed during wartime. This obviously brings up the question: Should the modern-day descendants of the Dakota tribe provide reparations for those innocent civilian descendants? Some may say this question is ludicrous, but it is a fair inquiry.

The last example is brief yet powerful. Should the descendants of the Barbary pirates (a Muslim race) be compelled, by the United Nations, to pay reparations to the descendants of every single European for their part in the European slave trade? If so, how would this monumental compensation be distributed?

The conversation of reparations is, again, a complex topic for some. However, from my perspective, it is quite simple. Human depravity has occurred for tens of thousands of years. Every single race and ethnicity has been brutalized in one way or another by different societies. The only fair way to go about life is to accept what happened in the past and treat people fairly, respectfully, and with dignity in the present and future. It is considered frustrating not to follow this simple trail of logic. Generational punishment is the antithesis of unfairness.

Settler Colonialism

Put simply, settler colonialism is the practice of procuring new land from smaller, less powerful governments or societies. The obvious example is the British sending colonies to the New World, with the first colony being named Jamestown. From the very beginning of America's settler conception to the present-day United States of America, there have been indigenous people who protest and speak out against the actions of the past and the present United States. Some believe America should acknowledge its blood-soaked past, and others, who are more radical, believe that decolonialism is the answer to past actions. In other words, there are rational people who just want to be heard by the current United States government, and there are others who want to completely transform America and replace it with a different totalitarian government, such as a communist-based society.

Rejecting Ancestral Compensation and Embracing Responsible Progress

Everybody has their opinion on this multifaceted topic. Everybody has their personal moral justifications to do certain things in order to bring about fairness. The correct answer is not made simple. However, we can conclude this topic as succinctly as possible.

Atrocities have happened in the past and have happened to everybody; these atrocities have been inflicted by every single race and endured by every single race. Demanding ancestral compensation to be paid out by current peoples is irresponsible and childish. Every society has colonized another, but we have learned from our ancestors' past actions. For example, the Sentinelese. The Sentinelese are a small group of people that live on Sentinel Island; it is untouched by modern hands, and it will never be touched by modern hands (unless nuclear war breaks out). The fact that this island will remain with no outside interference is an incredible spectacle. It is proof that humanity can, and will learn about the atrocities of the past and take specific actions according to the circumstances, like I plan to.

7

The True Republic: Exposing the Myths of Modern Democracy

In this moment of history, the political elite uses the term "democracy" to push the idea that America is a democratic system that advocates for equality and freedom. However, this is absolutely not true. America is a republic, where laws dictate the parameters of what Americans can and can't do. This is an incredible system if realized in the correct way. Democracy only leads to mob rule and inevitably dictatorship. If you look at the United Kingdom, you can see that it's completely falling apart because it runs on democracy instead of a righteous republic. If government systems are not implemented adequately, then you will be a slave. In my revolutionary plan, I will ensure that a republic is instilled and not bastardized by the hands of the political elite. My ambition sprouts from your eagerness to experience salvation. I am the only one in the modern world with the will to structure a government so that it runs fairly and punishes those who are truly evil.

Elizabeth Willing Powel asked a simple question directed toward Benjamin Franklin after the Constitutional Convention of September 18, 1787. She inquired, "Well, Doctor (Benjamin Franklin), what have we got, a republic or a monarchy?" In response, Benjamin Franklin proclaimed, "A Republic, ma'am, if you can keep it." Every American (and decent individual) is obligated to understand all different forms of government. These governments are categorized as the following: Monarchy (dictatorship), Oligarchy (elitists), Democracy (majority rules), Republic (law rules), and Anarchy (Government abolitionist). These different forms of government are very complicated to explain but can be boiled down to simple terms and actions performed by the top elites of whatever form of government a country decides upon (or is forced to be). For example, a country might be named one of the five forms of government listed above but will act in a way that represents a different government category. To be more specific, if you look at the "Democratic Republic of the Congo," one can infer (from the name) that this African-based country has the practices of a democratic republic. However, according to the Democracy Index, the "Democratic Republic of the Congo" is one of the most authoritarian regimes that exists in modern history. Another example is China. China is referred to as the "People's Republic of China," even though there is nothing republic about it; this country also scores on the Democracy Index as an authoritarian regime.

An Exploration of Constitutional and Absolute Power

In the simplest of terms, a monarchy is the governmental practice of having a head of state for life or until the abdication of the throne. Not all monarchies are dictatorships, but all dictatorships are monarchies or oligarchies. The difference in the amount of power delegated to the king, queen, or an individual with the equivalent title is defined by a government that subscribes to one of the following: constitutional monarchy or absolute monarchy. According to the book "Global Citizenship" by Jenny Wales (page 20), "A constitutional monarch holds the role of king or queen (or the equivalent) within the limits set out in the country's constitution. A constitution declares how the country will be run." With this definition, a constitutional monarchy is an individual limited by their constitution, similar to a presidency. Because these limits are in place, some argue that constitutional monarchies are the equivalent of a democracy or even a republic. An absolute monarchy is when a king, queen, or an individual with the equivalent title can make executive decisions despite any type of governmental advisory not to make a decision. Essentially, whoever is at the top of the absolute monarchy is able to do as they please, with no repercussions. These forms of monarchies are extremely rare in the modern era. According to thefreedictionary.com, there are only seven absolute monarchies in the modern world.

One of the very first constitutional monarchies to ever exist was that of the Hittites, an Anatolian Indo-European people from the Bronze Age. The Hittites had a king who was the supreme ruler of the encompassing kingdom, responsible for commanding military might, and judicial authority, as well as actively practicing high priest duties. However, even though the king had an immense amount of power, there were still some officials who exercised independent authority over various branches of the government. A fantastic example of this was the role of the Gal Mesedi (Chief of the Royal Bodyguards). Although the Gal Mesedi was subservient to the king, whoever took the mantle of Gal Mesedi was granted permission (by the king) to take executive and independent action during circumstances when the king wasn't directly available. King Telipinu, considered to be the last king of the Old Kingdom of the Hittites, reigned somewhere around 1500–1525 BC. He obtained power during a "dynastic power struggle." After seizing power, King Telipinu issued the Edict of Telipinus in order to address lawlessness and regulate royal succession. This edict entailed that the Pankus, the general assembly for the Hittite people, would be the new high court for constitutional crimes. These crimes would include murder, theft, vandalism, etc., which were observed and judged by the Pankus. The royal family, as well as the king himself, were also subject to jurisdiction under the Pankus.

When it comes to an absolute monarchy, there's no better example than the rise of the "Third Reich" or "Thousand-Year Reich." Prior to the National Socialist German Workers' Party, or Nazi party, Germany was referred to as the Weimar Republic, unofficially the German Republic. The Weimar Republic's name was derived from the central town in Germany called Weimar; this was where the constitutional assembly met. The reason the Germans drafted a constitution was to convert their system of imperialism to a democratic republic. However, because of massive destabilization due to social and economic factors, the fledgling democratic republic transitioned into a totalitarian dictatorship or an absolute monarchy. After Hitler rose through the ranks of the Nazi party, he ran against the war hero Paul von Hindenburg for president. Hitler obtained 36.8 percent of the vote, but since the German government was in shambles, the three successive chancellors failed to maintain control. This led to Hindenburg transferring power in late

January 1933 to 43-year-old Adolf Hitler. On January 30, 1933, the Third Reich was born.

When it comes to a constitutional monarchy, the benefits and disadvantages are the same as those of a democracy, republic, or a hybrid of the two. These benefits would include allowing the people to vote directly or through a representative in order to get certain laws passed. If a law is unconstitutional, there can be a vote to repeal said unconstitutional law. As for the royal family in charge of the government, they are subjected to the same laws that govern everybody else, making the system relatively fair. There are constitutional monarchies that don't have a constitution but have laws and agreements in place that act as a makeshift constitution. Two examples of this would be the United Kingdom and New Zealand. The disadvantage of a constitutional monarchy would be that the king, queen, or an individual with similar powers couldn't be elected out of office. The people could vote for politicians and representatives, but the royal family or oligarchy would permanently stay in power.

The advantages of an absolute monarchy are seldom beneficial. The classification of the benefit could lie in the absence of bureaucracy within that system. Whoever is the monarch could make a decision without having to go through anybody to put the decision into place. This would obviously cut back on time. Another benefit could possibly be rapid expansion, similar to Oda Nobunaga's monumental rise throughout ancient (15th century) Japan. The disadvantage of an absolute monarchy is the totalitarian reign aspect. Since there is no constitution, the monarch or dictator can break any laws that are imposed by said monarch or dictator. If they wanted to kill 1 million people because they felt that an uprising was imminent, then they could easily kill those people. An example of this was when

Joseph Stalin killed 37 government officials during August 1936 - March 1938. This event would be known as the "Great Purge."

A good example of a modern constitutional monarchy is Denmark. As of 2023, the current monarch is Margrethe II, who is beloved by her people and government. A good example of a modern absolute monarchy would be Saudi Arabia, with the current monarch being Salman bin Abdulaziz Al Saud. According to the Democracy Index, Saudi Arabia is classified as an authoritarian regime.

Balancing Tradition and Authority

A monarchy can have many faces. A constitutional monarchy supports law and the freedoms of people within the government. Nobody, including the king, queen, or someone of equivalent authority, can break the law or fabricate new laws without consulting different political parties. Constitutional monarchies are extremely similar to democracies, republics, or democratic republics. The only thing driving a wedge between monarchy, democracy, and republics is the presence of a royal family that cannot be removed from office. For example, before her death on September 8, 2022, Queen Elizabeth was the monarch of the United Kingdom for 71 years, far longer than any United States president.

An absolute monarchy is an antiquated authoritarian regime meant solely to suppress the people within that form of government. Regardless of the law, agreement, or understanding, the king, queen, or someone of equivalent authority can break the binding document and do as they please. The seven current absolute monarchies are Brunei, Oman, Jordan, Saudi Arabia, Bahrain, Kuwait, Qatar, and the United Arab Emirates.

It is extremely important to analyze the evolution of government. Whether it's a monarchy of some sort or a different form of government, it's up to the current generation to gaze upon the past and see what works and condemn what doesn't. Only then, individuals can start pursuing and sharpening current and future government systems that will benefit everybody and abandon antiquated regimes.

8

How International Trade & Capitalism Work Hand in Hand

I want to live in a country that represents the epicenter of freedom and security, whether that means walking down the street without being physically harmed or being allowed to open my own business. Capitalism represents freedom not only for our country but for the entire world. It is capitalism that has enriched poverty-stricken countries like China. It is capitalism that removes power from totalitarian dictatorships. It is capitalism that keeps the world safe from harm. The Marxists would like you to believe this isn't the case. Communists desperately want to strip away your freedom and enslave you so that you work for them without being able to gain any type of wealth. I am the future, and I will rain down vengeance on those governments who dare enslave their people. I will be the king who decides upon justice, for I am god-like. Globalization is the plan to spread American prosperity to all countries around the world, and anyone who dares stand in the way of this prosperity deserves to be cut down before me for not abiding by my splendid rule. For those who do not understand, I will explain in intricate detail.

Globalization is complicated when it comes to the layman. There are various subtleties when it comes to the concept, which can render the topic obscure and opaque. The simplest way of defining globalization is the international trade of goods and services, utilizing overseas corporations in order to produce said product or service; this being called economic interdependence. There are many reasons for a country to practice globalization. For example, after Mao Zedong's tyrannical communist tyranny was concluded, Deng Xiaoping, Former Chairman of the Central Military Commission of the People's Republic of China, implemented capitalist systems which eased tensions between the United States and China, and allowed for international trade to take place. This is just one of many examples of the benefits of globalization and partial, sometimes whole, capitalist conversion. Another way for international economic tranquility to take place is global citizenship.

Global citizenship, as explained in the book "The Practices of Global Citizenship" by Hans Schattle, is a multifaceted concept, which can either be interpreted as the pursuit of "political activism" by particular activists or the undying lust to further the understanding, or the expanding, of an individual's "cultural horizons" by pursuing international altruistic behavior. There are a lot more interpretations of what global citizenship represents, but unfortunately, some visages of the idea can harm or even destroy the economy.

Historical Perspective on Globalization

The earliest forms of trade and interaction among civilizations began very long ago. Indeed, commerce has been occurring since the time of Lucy, the first and oldest Australopithecus afarensis (human) ever to be discovered. However, perhaps an era where there was more documentation should be looked at. In the 16th century, but specifically in 1543, the introduction of firearms from Southeast Asia to Japan, as well as Tanegashima Island, took place. The introduction of guns to Japan was once believed to have happened because of European merchants or the accidental displacement of firearms due to crashed ships. However, this is apocryphal. The construction of extant examples of these old guns tells us that they came from Southeast Asia first, not anywhere else.

The introduction of firearms in Japan started off gradually. At first, individuals who came across and purchased guns used them for "hunting" or as "gifts." Soon after, "gunnery-masters" would trek across Japan, teaching various people how to fabricate gunpowder and use it in order to properly utilize the newly introduced firearms. "Gunnery-masters" also traded different types of gun technologies and techniques. Amazingly, it took more than a decade for firearms to be utilized in guerrilla campaigns and later wars. Eventually, Sengoku feudal lords established their own battalions of soldiers armed with guns.

Another very important form of trade was the introduction of coffee to Europe. The history of coffee begins in the 13th century, specifically in the geographical location of Ethiopia. Centuries from there, coffee was being slowly distributed to contiguous countries in Africa, like Egypt, Sudan, and

71

Eritrea. Around 300 years later, in 1615, coffee was finally introduced to Europe thanks to Venetian traders. However, Levant Rauwolf is ascribed to be the first European to ever drink coffee and write about his experience; these writings date back to between 1573 and 1576. The first printed reference to coffee appears as "chaube" in chapter viii of Rauwolf's Travels, with the context being the documentation of the manners and customs of the Aleppo people.

In 1652, coffee started to heavily affect England's economy for the best, with the opening of cafés. By 1700, there were roughly 2000 cafés officially open. These cafés were sometimes called "Penny Universities" because of the concentrated discussions about politics, religion, social ongoings, etc. that took place. Unfortunately, Charles II of England wasn't privy to the ongoings within these "Penny Universities." In retaliation, Charles II tried to ban these congregations in 1675, but after extreme protest, Charles II was forced to withdraw his sentiment. Cafés at this time would be a precursor to modern capitalism. Companies such as Lloyds of London, the British East India Company, and the London Stock Exchange began as cafés.

A funny piece of coffee history arose when in 1674, women wrote a petition against the coffee beverage, the petition being called "The Woman's Petition Against Coffee." Excerpts from the petition read as follows: "We find of late a very sensible decay of that true old English vigor; our gallants being every way so Frenchified...we can attribute to nothing more than the excessive use of that newfangled, abominable, heathenish liquor called coffee, which has so emasculated our husbands... and spend their money, all for a little base, black, thick, nasty, bitter, stinking, nauseous puddle-water... we humbly pray that henceforth the drinking of coffee may, on severe penalties, be forbidden and that instead thereof, lusty nappy beer and cock-ale... be recommended for general use." It's speculated that the reason why this anti-coffee movement occurred was because of the no-women-allowed policy in early cafés.

There are a lot of examples when it comes to early globalization, and let's be honest, a lot of it did have a harsh effect on the labor class at the time. The role of colonialism in shaping globalization is immense. A fantastic example is the Israeli-Palestinian Conflict. In 1000 B.C.E., the Kingdom of David is established, with Jerusalem as the capital. In 957 B.C.E., the first temple of Solomon is constructed in Jerusalem. Let it be known, at this time, it's roughly 1,600 years before the emergence of Islam. In 70 C.E., the Roman government invades Jerusalem to crack down on religious practice. The Jewish people retaliate by starting a revolt, but it is unsuccessful, and Jerusalem is destroyed. From 130 to 136 C.E., the Bar Kokhba revolt takes place, which was extremely damaging to the Roman Empire. In fact, the revolt was so damaging that the Roman Empire had to expend monumental amounts of resources to suppress the rebellion. After everything was said and done, around five years had passed. As an insult to the Jewish people, the Roman Empire renamed the area to Palestine. In the seventh century C.E., Islam is established, and Arabs take over Palestine in 636 C.E. From 1099 to 1291, the Crusaders take back the land, engaging in battles with the Islamic world, and establishing rule in Jerusalem and Israel. In 1291, the Crusaders are defeated by a Muslim group called the Mamluks, who rule for a few hundred years. In 1517, another Muslim empire, the Ottoman Empire, takes control. In 1897, the Zionist movement, created by Theodor Herzl, begins. In

1917, the Balfour Declaration is announced and passed on to the Zionist movement.

The colonialism that occurred for thousands of years in regards to Israel is the definition of exploiting a country in order to bolster foreign economic prosperity, and Israel is still under attack. It is only able to defend itself because of the United States sanctioning peace talks between Israel and various Muslim/Arab countries. For example, the Camp David Accords in 1979, the Oslo Accords in 1993, and the Abraham Accords in 2020. If it weren't for modern globalization techniques, who knows if Israel would still be standing at this point in time.

The American Industrial Revolution had a massive part to play when talking about (past and present) globalization. The year is debated amongst scholars from various walks of life, but the most common answer for when the Industrial Revolution started was 1750. The backbone of the Industrial Revolution is coal, oil, and natural gas, which have been entombed within the Earth for hundreds of millions of years. "345–280 million years ago," tens of millions of trees fell and littered the ancient ground. After a while, water would begin to cover these massive tree carcasses. Since the water was precluding oxygen and bacteria from coming in contact with the trees, they could not decay them. These trees would slowly sink into the ground, where an enormous amount of pressure would bear down on the foliage. Millions of years later, the compression turned them into dark, carbonic, ignitable rocks: coal.

Ever since the discovery, we, as a society, have been utilizing these naturally occurring agents to fuel our economy, as well as other international economies. For example, selling oil from the Strategic Petroleum Reserve to China. According to poynter.org, "Biden has authorized the sale of some of the reserve's crude oil to counteract supply shortages, notably the West's decision to cut back on Russian oil in the wake of its invasion of Ukraine. The process is done through a longstanding competitive bidding process, and whoever pays the most gets the oil." On April 21, 2022, the United States sold 950,000 barrels of oil to Unipec America, a Houston-based, Chinese-owned company. There have been some critics of this decision, most notably Tucker Carlson, who said, "So, as gas prices set records in this country, as American citizens who were born here and vote and pay taxes cannot afford to fuel their own cars, the Biden administration is selling off our emergency oil reserves to China." Take that as you will.

Another example is the Korea-U.S. Free Trade Agreement between the United States and The Republic of Korea (South Korea), which was implemented on March 15, 2012, and later amended in September of 2018. According to ustr.gov, "U.S. goods exports to Korea, South in 2019 were $56.5 billion, up 0.4% ($229 million) from 2018 and up 97.6% from 2009. U.S. exports to Korea, South are up 30.1% from 2011 (pre-FTA). U.S. exports to Korea, South account for 3% of overall U.S. exports in 2019." Countries that haven't experienced their own Industrial Revolution, or that are under Socialist/Communist tyranny, will be far inferior to countries that have gone through the industrial revolution, or countries that do not have a tyrant at its helm.

These post-Industrial Revolution International Trade Agreements (ITA) are all fun and good, but what did post-World War II globalization look like? Well, when it came to Japan, international trade and assistance played a significant role in Japan's rehabilitation. After Japan officially surrendered, with the bombardment on Nagasaki and Hiroshima playing a part in the capitulation, on Sept. 2, 1945, the United States stepped in to help Japan back into the international community by strengthening military, political, and economic ties. On Sept. 8, 1951, the San Francisco Peace Treaty was signed (going into effect on April 28, 1952), allowing for future globalization trade deals to exist.

The Economics of International Trade

As I stated prior, trade has existed for tens of thousands of years. To our ancestors, this form of exchange definitely enhanced the well-being of their antiquated communities. Usually, the head honcho (alpha) of the tribe or small community would be the commander and chief in every decision. Ergo, whoever was in charge would have been an ancient economist. Whether or not ancient man understood the ever-increasing importance of economics is up for debate, but they definitely benefited from domestic trade.

Thousands of years later, a man by the name of Benjamin Franklin would utter words more accurate than any economist before him: "No nation was ever ruined by trade." This sentiment has only been expanded upon, especially when talking about international trade. When discussing the evidence of success during the international trade process, it appears to be vast and only beneficial to nations who participate. Many nations have experienced an economic boom within the last several decades (for example, Japan, South Korea, China, and India) merely because they established globalization as a regulatory occurrence for bolstering their Gross Domestic

Product (GDP) output and to obtain monolithic levels of wealth (how that wealth is distributed is dependent on the economic makeup of the country). An earlier example reflects this extremely well. Deng Xiaoping, Former Chairman of the Central Military Commission of the People's Republic of China, implemented capitalist systems in order to save his purely Communist economy, aka an atrocious economy that has cost China "40 million deaths and perhaps 80 million or more" under Mao Zedong. Deng Xiaoping was so dedicated to the implementation of capitalist systems that he visited the United States on January 29, 1979, with then-President Jimmy Carter to discuss how capitalism worked and how it should be embedded in China. Ever since then, China has become the second-largest government in the world.

China's comparative advantage has now become extremely cheap labor, and more extremely cheap labor. Since the initial visit from Deng Xiaoping in 1979, China and the United States, where globalization is discussed, have been massive international trading partners. Unfortunately, this inexpensive form of labor comes at a terrible price, which is not monetary. The inconceivable amount of human rights violations that did, and still, take place is essentially palpable across oceans and other countries. The moral implications are obviously up for debate. Some would exclaim, "We need to cut off trade with China because of these human rights violations," and others would say, "This cheap form of labor is invaluable and a small price to pay." Let's not also forget about China's industrial global supply chain and its impact. Research pursued by Rhodium Group determined China emitted 27% of the world's greenhouse gases in 2019. Amongst other very terrible occurrences, this has led to the acid rain phenomenon.

According to the University of California Press, "Acid rain, defined as rainwater with a pH < 5.6, has become one of China's most prominent environmental problems (Marion, 1998; Seinfeld, 1998; Aas et al., 2007; Niu et al., 2014). The harm caused by acid rain includes soil acidification, degradation of the soil agricultural ecosystem, forest decline, and adverse health impacts (Bian and Yu, 1992; Menz and Seip, 2004; Rice and Herman, 2012; Zhu et al., 2016)."

Global Citizenship: Definition and Evolution

As defined by Hugh Evans, Global Citizenship is the ideology that individuals from different nations should treat each other as though they were a part of one big nation, called humanity. During the TED TALK, Mr. Evans gives various examples of how certain events in his life led him down a path of international advocacy. He talks about a trip he took to the Philippines, specifically a location called "Smokey Mountain." Petrified by the inhumane living conditions in Smokey Mountain, Mr. Evans collaborated with the rock band Pearl Jam and was successful in steering Kevin Rudd's (former Prime Minister of Australia) decision to double the budget of the GHD (Global Health and Development), adding $6.2 billion somewhere in the 2000s. However, this increase in funding amounted to nothing; after six years from the original budget increase, the money evaporated. In the framework of the TED TALK, a global citizen is defined as somebody who really wants to allocate resources to poor countries without understanding why these countries are poverty-stricken in the first place.

The evolution of what it means to be a global citizen varies from person to person. An individual may believe that, even though they are within their country, they would like to help other people in different countries. This is not a selfish ideology. In totalitarian countries, such as North Korea, people are oppressed and even slaughtered when stepping out of line. Even if you're just a tourist in one of these countries, you are subjected to their hellish regulations. Otto Frederick Warmbier is a perfect example of this. However, there is a large number of people who call themselves global citizens and wish to force their government to allocate resources to poorer countries, which in turn increases taxation on the populace. According to Hugh Evans, on a past MSNBC broadcast, the world governments need to commit $100 billion in climate financing for lower-income countries. This being stated, even though China makes up the majority of climate degradation. Mr. Evans also advocates for "$1 trillion in financing" for "countries in need through policy reforms at the world bank and other multinational development banks." Apparently, throwing money at a problem without understanding the situation is a valid stance to take. When talking about the evolution aspect of global citizenship, it all boils down to political advocacy or personal/general altruistic behavior.

The responsibilities of global citizens are extremely opinionated. Every single global citizen will give you a different answer. However, what seems to be the most obvious is reforming poverty-stricken governments by implementing capitalist systems or supplanting the previous economy with a purely capitalist economy. Obviously, it's not as simple as that, but shifting an incorrect government to a correct government would benefit the people within that system. For example, Hugh Evans talked a lot about the Philippines and Smokey

Mountain, but he doesn't talk about how the Philippines are still under the economic banner of Marxism (Marxism-Leninism-Maoism), which is a failed economic theory, right alongside every variant, as well as Socialism. In 1968, the communist faction of the Philippines was re-established. The communists proclaimed their goals were "the protracted people's struggle," modeled on Maoist China at the time. In 1972, the rebels' ranks enlarged after dictator Ferdinand Marcos declared martial law. Since the insurgency, around "150,000 combatants and civilians died." The insurgency of communist radicals has stunted economic development, especially in areas of the countryside where the rebels are most active. Obviously, there are more elements to this, but the fundamental fact is the Philippines is in the red because of these communist radicals. If their communist economy was supplanted by a capitalist economy, then national Philippine tranquility would begin to finally flourish.

This is the fundamental importance of properly understanding global citizenship. If an individual believes that throwing money at a problem, without understanding the actual cause, will fix anything, then they are mistaken. The correct way to be a global citizen is to advocate for these undeveloped countries to implement capitalist economies, as well as true democracies. On the individual level, people should donate to religion-based non-profits in order for these organizations to implement ground-level sanctuary to help and advocate for these foreign communities. This way, more powerful governments can be less involved with allocating resources (which will increase taxation among the populace) and more involved with advocating for an economic switch in these undeveloped nations.

The Interplay between International Trade and Global Citizenship

International trade fosters global interconnectedness through the transportation of materials and foreign human rights policies. The reason why global citizenship has become a massive talking point in recent years is because of the foul treatment by foreign governments toward their own people. If it weren't for industrial globalization, more individuals within their own country wouldn't gaze upon another country's treatment of their people as well as their policies to protect their people. Because of this ever-increasing view into other nations, fortunate people all around the world want to assist in any way they can. This is immensely important. Even though a nation's people should worry about the ongoing events within their country, it is also important to advocate for poverty-stricken countries to convert their antiquated systems into economic systems that have proven to be the new gold standard in the modern world.

It's extremely important for a government to be economically feasible and prosperous. However, this shouldn't come at the cost of their people's safety and hygiene. Yet, at the same time, the pursuit of global citizenship shouldn't hinder a country's progress. Achieving a balance between economic interests and global citizenship values is most important. How this can be done is still disputed. Whatever the decision, it's integral to be certain of a foreign nation's issues before trying to assist them.

Globalization with Responsibility

Globalization is a fundamental necessity when it comes to exporting and importing goods and services from across the world. Americans, Canadians, Mexicans, the Japanese, Laotians, etc., can't go a day without a cup of coffee, which originally came from Ethiopia. Some individuals will say that because certain atrocities from the past took place, this means you (as modern people) should not enjoy the modern commodity. Well, this is definitely correct when talking about antiquity. Atrocious actions did take place in order to bring coffee from Ethiopia to the contiguous countries in Africa, and then Europe, and then inevitably to the United States. Tens of thousands of slaves were forcibly put on coffee plantations in order to harvest coffee so antiquated people could ship the commodity to other countries. These actions by ancient people were irrefutably barbaric. However, their actions are set in stone, and the only way to look at their practices in maturity is to be vigilant for the warning signs so we, as current people, can hold countries that still participate in these atrocious actions responsible for their inhuman misconduct.

This is where global citizenship should come into play. Instead of throwing money at the problem and hoping it sticks, as Hugh Evans proposes, prosperous nations should advocate for these poverty-stricken countries to shift their economy into a capitalist one. This can be executed without utilizing billions of taxpayers' dollars or printing billions of dollars (which can dilute any currency). During this process of advocacy, individual citizens should donate some money to Christian-based non-profit organizations so groundwork in these countries can start to prosperously affect the inhabitants of these poverty-stricken countries. In this way, a lot more help can be allocated to these countries without degrading an individual's own country.

The future of globalization and global citizenship in an ever-changing world is up to governments and the people who reside in their government. We, as modern people, need to advocate for what works instead of being randomly, and naively, altruistic. It's strongly encouraged for people to be selfless and assist others, but if the principles from this behavior aren't instilled in more tyrannical governments, then random acts of altruism will be for naught.

9

Global Economic Development

America is 248 years old and is the freest and wealthiest country to ever exist in history. Our economic way of life is absolutely integral for the salvation of other countries. You, as a citizen, must take pride in the United States of America and in how hard our ancestors worked to turn mountains of dirt into cities of prosperity. After I enable America's consolidation, if other countries refuse to abide by our superior way of life, then they will experience my rage, which will reflect their people's screams of suffering; too many innocent people across the world have been butchered because of madmen's corrupt and disgusting ideologies. I know best when it comes to what works and what doesn't, and all I see around the world is insufficiency and tyranny. America is the epicenter, it is time for other countries to follow our high-ranking way of life.

In the simplest of terms, a "developed" country, or "more economically developed country" (MEDC), is a sovereign nation that has significant, advanced technological advancements, which improve the quality of life for its residents. An example of this concept would be post-World War II Japan.

When World War II officially ended on May 7, 1945, Japan still advocated for engagement against the United States and its allies. However, President Truman, in order to reduce the number of lives that would have been lost during a ground offensive, decided to drop two nuclear bombs on Nagasaki and Hiroshima. On September 2, 1945, Japan officially surrendered and signed the "Japanese Instrument of Surrender" document. With the signing of this agreement, Japan agreed to the occupation of its land by the United States.

From 1941 to 1945, the devastation that occurred in Japan was tremendously profound. There were nearly 2.8 million Japanese deaths, the nation's wealth depleted by 25%, hyperinflation took root, and commodity shortages plagued Japan. Shortly after the unconditional surrender, there were other extremely negative factors that occurred. One of them included radiation dispersal throughout the local ecosystem of Hiroshima and Nagasaki, which caused agonizing radiation-based deaths, as well as cursed newborns with permanent birth defects.

From 1945 through the 1960s, Japan began phase 1 of its economic bounce-back. Japan's main goal was to "catch up with North American and European industrial economies" by implementing a multitude of government-based initiatives that spurred the economy at a relatively quick pace. To provide an example, according to Prof. Akira Furukawa (Ritsumeikan University): "the (Japanese) government created a system to mobilize and direct funds to key industries for rapid economic development." This initiative certainly played a key role in the rehabilitation of Japan's economy and paved the way for Japan's economic titan status in modernity.

Along with industrial rehabilitation, the United States also encouraged Japan to enact various measures, including Zaibatsu dissolution, fair market rules, agricultural reform, labor market reform, education reform, and more. All of these new regulations were meant to lift up and assist the extremely damaged country, as well as increase the quality of life for the inhabitants of Japan. After years of implementation and certain strategic reforms enacted by the Japanese government, Japan has now become one of the freest and economically viable (oriental) countries on the planet, classifying it as a "developed country."

The concept (definition) of a "developing" country is hotly debated among economists and other experts on the development of countries. The simplest definition of a "developing" country is a country that struggles with industrial development, despite an abundance of resources, due to autocratic regimes seizing ultimate power over its people. This leads to the country's slow industrial innovation, which becomes stifled due to fear of extreme punishment. Again, this definition is hotly debated. Some believe that this definition is narrow-sighted, conveying that a country's classification as "developing" is incorrect and should be referred to as a newly emerging economy (NEE). However, the term NEE is used interchangeably with the term low and middle-income country (LMIC), which refers to lackluster economic growth and a low level of democracy. Some also believe the term "developing" country conveys an "us" and "them" approach, which can be seen as discriminatory. A perfect example of a "developing" country was post-Deng Xiaoping China.

Prior to Deng Xiaoping's implementation of capitalism, which saved China from Mao Zedong's atrocious economic policies, Mao Zedong's Great Leap Forward economic campaign was in full effect. Mao advocated for industrialization through forced labor, the Four Pests campaign (aimed at eradicating mosquitoes, flies, sparrows, and rats), the concept of Juche Works (encouraging workers to view their pain and suffering as beneficial for their country; Juche was established in North Korea but was also implemented during the Great Leap Forward), universal healthcare, and various other Communist programs. However, after the death toll reached 36 million, Mao Zedong was replaced by Li Shaoqi in 1959. This decision was short-lived because in 1966, Mao Zedong regained his position as Chairman by blaming the bourgeoisie for the millions of deaths. The Chinese people believed Mao, and trust was reestablished. To control the bourgeoisie, Mao Zedong encouraged the young generation to suppress anyone critical of the Chinese Communist Party; these youths were known as the Red Guard or Communist revolutionaries. The Red Guard were so loyal to Mao that they would murder professors critical of communism and participate in "flash banquets" (ritualistic cannibalism) as a fear-mongering tactic for those not loyal enough. When everything was said and done, and Mao Zedong passed away, the death toll had risen to 65 million (this figure coming from The Black Book of Communism by Stéphane Courtois).

Beyond just examples and elaboration, I will delve into the very foundation of "developed" and "developing" countries to extrapolate the true meaning behind the terminologies. Also, the discussion of climate change will be integrated within the concepts of "developed" and "developing" countries as a way to elaborate on how country economies, conservation methods, and policies impact the local ecosystem. To convey sincerity, when discussing certain countries that have lackluster climate change prevention initiatives, the type of language that will be utilized will be sharp, direct, and poised. This is in order to be as respectful as possible in connection to the environment. However, don't let this be confused with blind allegiance toward climate change activism. The most important thing to focus on when it comes to the climate, as well as the world itself, is to ensure that global superpowers are responsible and not driven by homicidal intentions. The worst thing that can happen to our planet, which includes the many ecosystems that reside on it, is to ensure that nobody hits the big red button and unleashes nuclear warfare. In short, international relations need to take precedence before acting on any type of conservation treaty.

Defining Developed and Developing Countries

In order to be crystal clear when it comes to the discussion of the definition of "developed" and "developing" countries, the classification will be described in layman's terms. A "developed" country is a nation that is fully independent from any other nation. This would include not requiring assistance economically, on the humanitarian front, and being free to rule within its own sovereignty without any restraints. A "developing" nation is a country that needs a decent amount of assistance on all fronts in order to survive or have its inhabitants prosper (or, at the very least, not suffer excruciatingly). Unfortunately, a multitude of "developing" nations are authoritarian and rank low on the democracy index. This is important because if a country has leadership that is dictatorial, then the tyrant will fulfill their own needs rather than the needs of their people, which will end up putting the country in a stranglehold and halt any type of meaningful development. A perfect example would be the inhabitants of the Gaza Strip.

Without getting too involved in the Israel-Palestine conflict, which would be beyond scope, it must be said that the Palestinian leadership, Hamas (the terrorist organization), is putting a stranglehold on its people when it comes to any type of development. Instead of utilizing resources that have been gifted to them by the European Union (for example, "€100 million" into pipeline projects), Hamas rips the material out from under the ground and re-lathes it into "homemade rockets" to fire upon Israel. Obviously, this leads to bloody strife between the two; strife that could be avoided if Hamas stopped attempting to eradicate the Jewish people. Even though this is an extreme example of a "developing" country, or in this case a government facing extreme recession, any type of autocratic regime, no matter how massive, can be classified as a developing nation. China would be a perfect example.

In short, the Chinese government has been facing severe cases of acid rain in certain provinces. According to Guilin Han and Rui Qu (from the Elementa: Science of the Anthropocene), "The chemical composition of rainwater in the southern and northern cities of China has changed significantly in recent decades. According to the China Statistical Yearbook (National Bureau of Statistics of the People's Republic of China, 2018), the cities showed significant SO_2 and NO_x concentration variations, resulting in discrepancies in the chemical composition of rainwater. Still, we observed a general trend in the chemical composition throughout the decades. Generally, a decline in pH occurred mainly in the late 1990s to mid-2000s, resulting in acid rainwater across China."

Even though China is considered a massive superpower, that still doesn't conclude the conversation on whether or not China should be considered a "developing" nation. Again, not to bring up topics that are beyond the scope, but if we look at the atrocious one-child policy, which was enforced by China, the country is clearly struggling economically; there aren't enough young people in comparison to older people. This will obviously have extremely drastic effects going into the future.

Developed Countries and Global Warming

According to Jenny Wales (in Global Citizenship - Student Book), "The Chinese government decided that things had to change. No new coal-fired power stations were built, and older ones were shut down. In some cities, such as Beijing, the number of cars on the road was restricted. 'New energy vehicles' (NEVs) have become very popular in China, such as electric buses - China has more than 400,000, or about 99 percent of the world's total! The government also introduced the 'Great Green Wall' program, which aims to restore the environment by planting trees. So far, 35 billion trees have been planted to prevent deserts from taking over farmland. The hope is that the trees will improve the soil quality and allow food crops to grow around them."

Judging from the quote, it is safe to assume that the author believes that there is green progress occurring in China. However, according to Tian-tian Feng (Doctor of Technology Economics and Management, School of Humanities and Economic Management at the University of Geosciences, Beijing, China), "For China, greenhouse gas emissions increased by 0.075 gigatons

(Gt) in the period of 1995–2000 and increased by 4.23 Gt from 2000 to 2009, then reached the amount of 8.61 Gt in 2009." From this information, greenhouse gas emissions released into the (Chinese government's) atmosphere are equivalent to 17,220 pounds, and to this day, the government is still releasing more and more greenhouse gas emissions into the atmosphere. According to bloomberg.com, "China alone generated about the same amount of CO_2 as the next four (greenhouse gas emission runner-up) countries combined."

This is obviously a severe problem and demonstrates that the Chinese government may proclaim they are doing everything they can to limit greenhouse gas emissions, but they are not actually implementing any type of durable solution that is economically feasible. This cannot go on. These emissions, which are extraordinarily dangerous in high quantities/conce ntrations, are the sole reason why the acid rain phenomenon is still a massive issue within certain provinces.

The United States of America also emits its fair share of greenhouse gases. In 2021, "6,340.2 million metric tons of carbon dioxide" were released into the atmosphere. Even though China releases double the amount of greenhouse gas emissions into the atmosphere, Americans still need to be conscious of the amount of fossil fuel emissions being released. One solution that has been put forward in the political discourse is the push for nuclear power. Since nuclear power doesn't generate negative emissions, some people of certain political persuasions see nuclear power as a possible contender for sustainability.

Developing Countries and Global Warming

Russia, classified as a country in "Transition" by investope-dia.com, holds the fourth global rank when it comes to greenhouse emissions. As of 2021, Russia is credited with emitting around 3.45 billion tonnes of greenhouse gas emissions per year. Of this total, 40.64% comes from fossil fuel operations, 24.37% from power-related operations, and 12.62% is directly from the manufacturing process. According to Daisuke Kitade (from the Mitsui & Co. Global Strategic Studies Institute), "In the future, legislation for a Carbon Border Adjustment Mechanism (CBAM) will be developed, and public opinion in Russia on climate change risk may increase, leading to a shift in the Russian government's climate change measures towards a more decarbonization-oriented approach."

In other words, Russia aims to become completely carbon neutral by the year 2060 and will use CBAM legislation to achieve this goal. However, considering the Ukraine-Russia war, the likelihood of Russia decreasing their greenhouse gas emissions by finding alternative methods of energy output is slim. War is the ultimate consumer of carbon-based emissions, so this plan will most likely fail (the 2060 carbon neutrality plan is public relations propaganda). The only viable method to reduce greenhouse gas emissions while sacrificing large amounts of power is to utilize nuclear energy power plants.

Brazil is another country classified as a "developing" nation, currently in seventh place for greenhouse gas emissions. Brazil is also recognized as "the largest greenhouse gas emitter in the Latin America and Caribbean region." According to US-AID, "Brazil updated its Nationally Determined Contribution (NDC) in April 2022 for the second time, not identifying sector-specific goals. Emissions reduction goals for 2025 and 2030 were included, noting a long-term objective of carbon neutrality by 2050 and plans to stop illegal deforestation by 2028. Significant efforts will be required to achieve zero deforestation."

Efforts to Bridge the Economic Gap

There have been many actions and proposals brought forth by the United Nations, as well as various world superpowers, to reduce greenhouse gas emissions from carbon-related fuel sources. Proposals like the "Green New Deal" and "The Paris Agreement" have been drafted and partially implemented. However, the majority of these actions and proposals are fundamentally flawed and unrealistic. For example, for the Green New Deal to work, there would need to be a drastic increase in taxes and a comprehensive solution for the winter months of the year. If all energy production were to freeze, there would be more consumption than there is production, and all electrical sources would shut down (unless fossil fuels are implemented). There is a possibility to implement renewables while matching, and potentially even surpassing, carbon-based power, and that is nuclear energy plants. According to Richard Rhodes, an American historian, "Rather than chemical burning, it generates baseload electricity with no output of carbon, the villainous element of global warming. Switching from coal to nuclear power is radically decarbonizing, since nuclear power plants release greenhouse gases only from the ancillary use of fossil fuels during their construction, mining, fuel processing, maintenance, and decommissioning – about as much as solar power." The only caveat to nuclear power is the potential for a nuclear meltdown, which has been known to cause massive damage to organic ecosystems; for example, the Fukushima nuclear accident in Japan in 2011.

Besides ambitious fuel and power reforms, proposals like The Paris Agreement have been created in order to promote international economic development and security. The method that would be employed is to accumulate a large amount of money and disperse it into poor nations, with the theory being that it would bolster the nation's wealth. However, this tactic can be detrimental to participating nations putting forth this large amount of money. Where would this money be coming from? Obviously, the taxpayer within that nation, or participating countries would have to print more money and allocate these newly printed funds to the United Nations, which would then disperse the money to the poor nations. This idea will have adverse long-term effects on any participating country. There are many more ideas that have been put forward, but none of them have panned out according to the stipulations within the proposed document, with the exception of nonprofit, third-party, organizations allocating donated resources to struggling countries.

Critique of Global Economic Intervention and Classification Systems

The whims of the philanthropic will be crushed under economic insufficiency and erratic saviorism. The United Nations and they are un-calculated experimentation will fall through for the sheer fact that they cannot enforce anything as well as not draft a piece of legislation that is not completely ludicrous on the economic frontier. Unless, for some reason, the higher-ups at the United Nations experience some type of voyeurism in relation to the outcome of their terrible decisions, they are naïve octogenarians with no comprehension of their actions because of their far removal from reality; that's not to say there's no malignant behavior, considering the United Nations decreed that there should be a cease-fire between Israel and Palestine even though the Palestinian terrorist organization, Hamas, killed 1,500 innocent people.

The classification of a country being "developed" and developing" is dubious, but not for the reasons some may assume. If a country is classified as one of the two options the United Nations, or different organizations and governments, will attempt to implement restrictions or advocations. When it comes to "developed" countries they will be pressured in full by means of extrapolating more money from its inhabitants or printing more money in order to allocate the funds to the World Bank; where dissemination will take place. This would irrevocably damage any government that participates. This is because the whole concept of allocating monetary resources in order to bolster another nation's GDP is communist. Nothing can destroy a country as thoroughly as communism.

In relation to a "developing" country, the more money that's

95

given, the more complacency there will be in that poorer government. This is extremely damaging because this type of monetary allocation incentivizes autocratic regime behavior. If the government terrorizes its own people, leading to economic stagnation, and the United Nations bails them out by drafting legislation that encourages richer countries to donate monetary funds to the "developing" country, then there is significant incentivizing of tyrannical behavior because of the lack of punishment or forceful reform.

The two classifications of "developed" and "developing" are completely unnecessary and backward thinking. There should only be two classifications for countries: just and authoritarian. When it comes to authoritarian countries, their system needs to be supplanted with capitalism and true democracy or a constitutional republic. As for just civilizations, they need to encourage this change while not allocating monetary resources. That job should be left up to third-party organizations. This is to ensure the economy doesn't suffer due to over-taxation and excessive printing of money.

There needs to be more research when it comes to helping autocratic countries convert into just countries. The conversion process isn't as black-and-white as someone may conclude but is extremely complicated because of all the small elements that need to be taken into consideration. However, once the formula has been developed, this type of conversion process needs to be implemented immediately; otherwise, global progress will always plateau.

10

Is There Merit to the Democratic Anthropocene Hypothesis?

Humans are the most superior creatures to ever evolve on this planet. However, this superiority should not breed arrogance within the population of our country. Even though it is extremely important for fossil fuels to be utilized to drive progress, there needs to be a way to pivot from fossil fuels to alternative sources of energy, such as nuclear energy. Because of weak Marxist international policies (pushed by the United Nations), smaller countries are not able to industrialize and provide necessary resources to their populations. These small countries need to industrialize while simultaneously adopting our superior philosophy. Once they are satisfactorily converted, they should be given access to alternative energy sources like nuclear power. It is extremely important for international countries to adopt our ideology, especially to avoid situations like Iran having nuclear capabilities without the correct moral framework installed within their government.

The Anthropocene is a complicated topic because it is relatively new. I will try to explain it as clearly as possible so that everyone can understand what it is and why it's important. Additionally, it must be emphasized that current policy proposals related to the Anthropocene are ludicrous and disgustingly wretched.

The Anthropocene, or the "recent age of man," is an unofficial archaeological concept that was first introduced by American biologist Eugene Stoermer in the 1980s but made popular by Dutch chemist and Nobel laureate Paul Crutzen in 2000. Only recently has the term Anthropocene become recommended to the International Commission on Stratigraphy to be classified as an official nomenclature that encapsulates human industrialization. There is a large debate within the scientific community about when the Anthropocene commenced. However, certain scientists agree with the notion that the Anthropocene began during the Industrial Revolution. For example, Paul Crutzen believed the epoch began around 1784, coinciding with James Watt's invention of the steam engine. Whatever future determination is used is irrelevant. The human effect on planet Earth is noticeable not only on the surface level but also on the geographical level.

According to David B. Kemp, Peter M. Sadler, and Veerle Vanacker's study, which highlights the human impact on North American erosion, alluvium accumulation rates have skyrocketed since 200 years ago, which proves how human actions have influenced sediment transfer and storage on a geological scale. Human activity is embedded within the Earth, and it's not going to disappear anytime in the near future. Look no further than the Waste Isolation Pilot Plant (WIPP), near Carlsbad, New Mexico. WIPP is a nuclear waste storage facility, which deals with the cleanup operations of nuclear tests and the waste of nuclear plants. Nuclear waste, albeit not as dangerous as it's made out to be by the media, is still capable of being radioactive for thousands, tens of thousands, or even hundreds of thousands of years. No matter somebody's views on nuclear energy, the waste is going to stick around for a very long time.

Challenges of a Democratic Anthropocene

Jedediah Britton-Purdy asserts that humanity has to imagine a democratic Anthropocene by utilizing "Amartya Sen's famous observation that no famine has ever taken place in a democracy." This idea is extremely bold, even for an individual who has made it their life's mission to bring awareness to humans' effect on planet Earth. According to an EJDR article titled "The Merits of Democracy in Famine Protection – Fact or Fallacy?," the relationship between democracy and famine prevention is more complex than Sen's hypothesis, indicating that other factors besides the political system play significant roles in famine occurrences. Therefore, Amartya Sen's extrapolation isn't fully accurate when considering other significant factors. This is important because humanity cannot base its survival or integral policies (that will drain the wealth of countries) on not fully realized concepts. This would be irresponsible.

In relation to the food movement, Jedediah Britton-Purdy exclaims, "The food movement provides a possible model of the next politics of nature, emphasizing the metabolism between humans and the world." In the modern sense, growing food traditionally will be extremely insufficient in the long term. Scientists have realized this and have begun the process of cloning cultured animal cells in order to create fully realized consumable food products. According to the FDA, through various scientific methods, the process of cloning animal cells in order to feed populations has already occurred. After the cloning process, the cells, or synthesized meat, will be "prepared using conventional food processing and packaging methods" while abiding by the Federal Food, Drug, and Cosmetic Act. If this method of food production were to expand, then the problem of a possible famine would dissipate among third-world countries and others.

The practice of producing energy is also capable of man-made evolution. To exclaim and demand the removal of fossil fuel usage is irresponsible when taking into account that lesser developed countries need the energy of fossil fuels to sustain their societies. Several smaller countries within modernity are experiencing, for the very first time, their own industrial revolution. To deprive these nations of their energy via global policies of environmental altruism is to plateau their progress. However, this isn't to say the practice of utilizing fossil fuels shouldn't be slowly supplanted in favor of another power source. Nuclear energy is the future when it comes to sustainable and clean energy. However, it still obtains a bad perception from the public because of incidents like Chernobyl, Fukushima, and the nuclear bombs from World War II. According to the Columbia Climate School, "nuclear power is the second-largest source of clean energy after hydropower," with a significant decrease in the amount of harmful emissions in comparison to solar energy and the current standardized fossil fuels. This idea is supported by a study titled "Understanding future emissions from low-carbon power systems by integration of life-cycle assessment and integrated energy modeling," by conveying to the reader that a kilowatt-hour of nuclear-generated electricity only produces

4 grams of CO_2 in comparison to coal, which emits 109 grams of CO_2 for the same duration. The amount of CO_2 emissions is reduced by approximately 96.33%.

Although the implementation of nuclear power would be beneficial to humanity when it comes to reducing the amount of CO_2 emissions, it has to be considered that some nations would utilize this power for nefarious actions rather than supporting their own population. A perfect example of a nation utilizing nuclear power for nefarious purposes would be late 1970s to the 1980s Iraq, with Saddam Hussein pursuing nuclear energy in order to eviscerate Israel via a nuclear salvo. A more modern example of a nation that would utilize nuclear power for pure destruction would be Iran. Unfortunately, Iran's nuclear program was bolstered by the Obama Administration's funded Iran Nuclear Deal, which was strategically left behind by the Trump Administration.

Globally democratizing the Anthropocene, as described by Jedediah Britton-Purdy, would be extremely dangerous to the overall welfare of humanity. Democracy, as a concept, sounds pleasing to the ears, but history has taught humanity that a pure democracy can lead to emotionally passionate uprisings by the majority of a country, potentially resulting in its destruction via revolution. This is a dilemma. Humans are creatures of emotion and passion, and if that passion becomes too strong, then destruction is imminent. Our founding fathers understood this; which is why James Madison, one year before attending the Constitutional Convention, studied tirelessly on the history of failed democracies to craft a constitution that would enable long-term unity. Within the American constitution, nowhere does it say the word democracy, only republic. As a society, we must build upon our founding fathers' knowledge by pursuing a republican-style Anthropocene. That way, nuclear power won't fall into the hands of the corrupt and malignant, but only into the hands of the righteous and fair.

Monetary Concerns

The concept of equity, and its practice, on an economic scale is fairly dubious. If individuals, or countries, obtain resources in relation to combating climate change from another country, will that nation be able to support itself in the long term? This question was asked when the Green New Deal was proposed. The Green New Deal was a very controversial bill that would have attempted to decrease the amount of carbon emissions. However, according to the American Action Forum, the annual cost of ensuring these decreases would have amounted to nearly $10 trillion, eclipsing most countries' GDPs. This type of cost is unreasonably expensive and would only serve to further bankrupt the United States. Not only that, but living conditions for the average American family would decrease significantly, leading to widespread chaos and resentment toward the government. Thankfully, Representative Alexandria Ocasio-Cortez and Senator Ed Markey's proposal to Congress failed, and the Green New Deal was consigned to the ash heap of history.

Another example of an outrageously burdensome agreement that would impede economic progress for the United States is the Paris Agreement. Just like the Green New Deal, the Paris Agreement advocates for the decrease of carbon emissions that would permeate through the atmosphere. However, the major caveat to the concept is the outrageous price tag.

According to a study by the Heritage Foundation, adhering to the regulations stemming from the Paris Agreement could lead to substantial job losses, a considerable decrease in family income, a significant reduction in the U.S. GDP, and increased household electricity expenditures. In other words, abiding by the Paris Agreement isn't economically feasible.

In the case of employing equity, it's just not possible to utilize when it comes to distributing resources to smaller nations, when those exact same nations could exploit their own naturally occurring resources in order to industrialize. It's almost like bigger countries are attempting to immerse themselves with altruism at the expense of their own people; similar to having a narcissistic saviorism mentality. Not only that, but if smaller countries don't industrialize and only subsist off of the handouts by bigger nations, then those smaller nations will become implicit in their own economic plateau and possible regression into antiquation; it's a bad deal for everybody.

Neoliberalism's Impact

As described by the Corporate Finance Institute, "Neoliberalism is an economic philosophy that conceptually describes a move towards free markets, capitalism, and a diversion from government ownership. The typical policies associated with neoliberalism include free trade, globalization, privatization, and changes in government spending to stimulate the private sector." Provided this definition, neoliberalism is extremely close to conservatism; some could even say the ideals are nearly identical, with the exception of how small the government should be and how certain social policies are implemented. However, when discussing the concept of neoliberalism, the conversation of wokeism and democratic socialism needs to be incorporated (because of the hostile takeover of the concept of liberalism).

The classic liberals of the past—John F. Kennedy, Bill Clinton, Jimmy Carter, etc.—believed in much of what modern conservative Republicans believe in. In his 1995 State of the Union address, former President Bill Clinton expressed his concerns over the amount of illegal immigrants pouring across the southern border and emphasized that the border needed to be secured so only law-abiding immigrants could come to America. This rhetoric is nearly identical to former President Donald Trump's ideals when it comes to securing the border. Look no further than former President Donald Trump's speech at the US-Mexico border in Eagle Pass, Texas.

However, some of the more up-and-coming radical left Democrats have made it clear on several occasions that they don't want a secured border. They believe that America should be reminiscent of a global transit center, rescuing foreigners from whatever problems they articulate, even if falsified. Representative Alexandria Ocasio-Cortez has stated several times that she believes the American border should be open for "human mobility." She has described America's immigration system as unjust and has highlighted the need to acknowledge human rights regardless of one's documentation status. AOC still believes in this concept even though, according to the Heritage Foundation, "Since Biden took office, over 6.2 million illegal aliens have been encountered at the nation's borders, and over 2 million of them have been released into the nation's interior. A considerable number of them have engaged in criminal activities once they settled. In 2023 alone, Border Patrol agents have encountered thousands of illegal aliens with prior criminal convictions, including assault, rape, and murder. The true extent of crimes committed by illegal aliens remains unknown because there are also over 1.5 million unaccounted for 'gotaways' since Biden's term began."

This radical-left philosophy (which encompasses more than just the border issue) needs to be kept in mind when possibly implementing Anthropocene policies. It's quite possible, as seen with the Green New Deal and Paris Agreement, that radical leftists will attempt to bankrupt America in order to pursue narcissistic altruism. Not only that, but it appears that there is a vitriolic hatred toward conservative, and even liberal, Republicans, which will lead to ad hominem attacks rather than logically inspired productive debates. If America wants to attempt to salvage the very unique ecosystem on earth, then the only way to do that is if there are policies which follow Republican-style governance.

Technological Innovation vs. Neo-environmentalism

Environmentalism and conservation efforts are not bad. Former President Theodore Roosevelt, often considered the "conservationist president," was an avid hunter of animals but within his private diaries lamented the decrease in animal populations and ecosystem detriment at the hands of humans. Because of this alternative perspective, considering the time period, former President Roosevelt made it one of his missions to preserve America's beautiful landscapes and animal populations. However, in conjunction with this conservation mentality, the American industrial revolution was still in full swing.

Within modernity, neo-environmentalists are more akin to fascists who attempt to redact speech and advocate for violent militant groups. For example, in late November 2023, Greta Thunberg gave a speech on climate change when a man suddenly walked on stage declaring, "I come here for a climate demonstration, not a political view." The man was referring to Greta Thunberg's solidarity with the terrorist group Hamas. Immediately after the interruption, Greta Thunberg started chanting, "No climate justice on occupied land." This chant obviously advocates for terrorism, considering at that moment in time it had only been one month before October 7 when Hamas terrorists entered Israel and started raping women, slaughtering men, and burning babies within their cribs. Not only that, but the incorrect notion that Israel is occupied land is categorically inaccurate in relation to history. The climate activists of today are not climate activists at all, and if America, as well as other countries, don't realize this soon, then not only will moral degradation continue, but the very real issue of environmental pollution won't be mitigated.

Harnessing Nuclear Power

A Democratic Anthropocene would be an absolute nightmare if the concept made it to policy. A better way to handle the increasing technological revolution in relation to the CO_2 emissions certain processes emit would be to completely adopt the power of nuclear energy as well as implement a republican form of government. However, for a republican form of government to work, we need it to be based on a universal morality (that would be rooted in observable/scientific analysis and not religious superstition), which everyone would follow, so the great power of nuclear energy won't be used for malignant reasons.

11

Human's Fragility-Conscience Over AI

To build a house, you must embed nails in the wood, and to do that, you must use a hammer. Ever since the dawn of man, technology has been integral to the development of modern society. For ancient humans to hunt, they needed to construct spears to take down large prey. For fledgling countries, industrialization was necessary to fabricate highly advanced machinery. Today, it is time to implement the wondrous technology of artificial intelligence. Advancement is the only way to become more relevant in the intergalactic empire that we, the human species, will construct in unison. Certain octogenarians and neo-environmentalists want to completely stop the hammer that will assist the human species in crafting a mighty feat of architecture. I will completely shred any semblance of power these brainless anti-humanists have over the current establishment so we can achieve the greatness we were always meant to inflict on our planet and universe.

While the technology still needs some work, artificial intelligence is advancing at an incredible rate. Some see this advancement as terrifying, while others view it as a revolutionary tool that can be used to quell hardships and boost productivity and innovation. However, no matter an individual's perception, artificial intelligence is knocking at mankind's front door, and there is nothing anyone can do to stop it. As a species on this planet, we are on the cusp of greatness—the next stage in human evolution.

To stick with our modern times, artificial intelligence has made it possible to minimize pseudo-information that has emerged due to bad/malignant forces. For example, on February 19, 2024, two videos were uploaded to the social media platform X, formerly known as Twitter. The first one depicted an elderly man slapping a lady who was shouting in his face. This video would have caused a massive uproar if it weren't for the second video, which was uploaded in the same post. The extended version of the first video was displayed and provided context to the assault. In this extended cut, the lady in the video slapped the elderly man after making remarks about his race. The elderly man retaliated by slapping her back, which led to the lady slapping him once again.

This is a perfect example of artificial intelligence (Community Notes or the X crowdsourced mechanism) being utilized to decrease the amount of false information disseminated through the internet. When the original shortened video clip was released on X, the community notes function immediately mobilized and provided context. This would lead to millions of users knowing the truth instead of being emotionally duped.

Even though thousands of videos and text-based information are being corrected through various different artificial intelligence methods, there are still concerns over AI being utilized for nefarious purposes without any countermeasures. Deep fakes of individuals would be a perfect example of this. Since a human deep fake is created through the consistent analysis of high-resolution faces, even artificial intelligence has a hard time distinguishing between the real deal and the simulated. A perfect example of this would be the deep fake of Volodymyr Zelenskyy, which was disseminated during the very beginning of the Russian-Ukraine war. In the deep fake video, Volodymyr Zelenskyy announces to Ukraine his surrender to Vladimir Putin. Fortunately, the deep fake of Volodymyr Zelenskyy wasn't passable as fully human. However, concerns of a higher quality deep fake are prevalent in the political zeitgeist.

Besides the espionage that has and will take place in the future through the advancement of artificial intelligence, AI is extremely prevalent in medicine, entertainment, and transport, as well as various other facets of life.

Critique of Current AI Research Focus

In terms of Anthropology, the effects of Artificial Intelligence are not sufficiently understood. Similar to research related to biology, such as gain-of-function research, artificial intelligence needs to be studied in a precise and meticulous manner. If a researcher or scientist opens Pandora's box, there might be no way of stopping the outcome. This is why extreme levels of precaution and restriction are placed upon researchers. For example, if an artificial intelligence researcher wants to apply for funding in academia, that individual will have to go through some type of ethics guidelines or review board; at Stanford University, this is called the Ethics and Society Review (ESR). Unfortunately, at the moment, this is not universal, but in some cases, it is mandatory for a researcher to implement an impact statement which clarifies how their research might negatively and positively impact society.

In terms of artificial intelligence research, the scope is exceptionally narrow. AI is primarily subsidized by massive corporations which have specific interests in natural language processing, computer vision, robotics, AI ethics, and more. This is not necessarily a bad occurrence. If a company grows sufficiently and decides to fund artificial intelligence research, then they should have every right to do so as long as the researchers involved follow the proper ethical precautions. As for government research relating to AI technology, the same prerequisites should be applicable. Legislators need to understand AI technology in order to adequately craft laws to keep potential bad actors in check.

In recent years, there have been a lot of individuals fearful that their jobs will be taken over by robots and artificial intelligence. This is not necessarily a bad practice when talking about blue-collar jobs. In 2020, there were approximately 415,000 police-reported crashes in relation to truck drivers; 4,444 of these being fatal crashes. In 2021, this number increased by 17% (5,788 fatal crashes). These statistics are contrasted by self-driving vehicle crash and fatality statistics. In 2023, there were approximately 612 self-driving car crashes in California, with 17 reported fatal incidents since May 2022. Human life is extremely precious, and any fatalities should not be taken lightly, but accidental deaths related to blue-collar work are extremely prevalent in America. So much, in fact, that it is extremely concerning. If blue-collar workers were supplanted with AI-driven vehicles, there will, of course, be incidences involving crashes and fatalities. However, there would be a lot less.

The pointless loss of human life can be mitigated with AI technology. For those who are worried about the loss of jobs, this shouldn't be a major concern. If more truck drivers were replaced with artificial intelligence, then there would, of course, be a loss of truck driver jobs relating to humans behind the wheel. However, these individuals will not lose their income. Blue-collar workers can transition into white-collar workers and potentially make even more money than they were making via STEM field occupations.

AI's Role in Minimizing Civilian Casualties in War

Over the years, the terrorist group, Hamas, has repeatedly launched rockets into Israel in order to kill as many Jewish Israelis as possible. These attacks are of the equivalency of more than 100 9/11s since 2006. In order to minimize casualties, Israel crafted a very sophisticated system titled "Iron Dome" in order to accomplish Israeli civilian safety. The artificial intelligence utilized is capable of tracking missiles fired by Hamas and colliding into them via real-time calculations. As Ben Shapiro conveys, it's of the equivalency of hitting a "bullet with a bullet" with only 90 seconds warning time. This type of defense is remarkable and has prevented countless lives from being taken by the terrorist organization. However, there are some flaws when it comes to Iron Dome. If there are too many rockets fired into Israel, then the system will not be able to calculate and target every single missile. This is a problem that's being slowly remedied by gradual updates to the system.

For whatever reason, if a global war happens, then this Iron Dome technology would be indispensable in protecting countless lives from hostile nations. Artificial intelligence, although not perfect, is still an adequate measure for defensive and offensive war.

Human-Cybernetic Symbiosis

Nearly every person in America has heard of the saying science fiction, but how many people believe that it's actually possible with modern science? Would the American people find this favorable? What about a brain interface that would allow individuals with severe brain or spinal trauma to experience normalcy again? Would people find this helpful... or dystopian? Unfortunately, "dystopian" is correct when referring to the Pew Research Center. According to an article titled "AI and Human Enhancement: Americans' Openness Is Tempered by a Range of Concerns," 56% of those surveyed believed cybernetic implants would be more detrimental than the supposed benefits. However, this perception could be marred due to Hollywood and various science fiction films that portray cybernetic implants in a less-than-favorable light. The Terminator and RoboCop franchises are perfect examples of entertainment misleading the American public, having them believe in a less-than-favorable outcome with no tangible evidence to go along with it.

Outside of Hollywood, cybernetics have proven themselves time and time again to be extremely beneficial to individuals who suffered an unfortunate accident. According to a Canadian newspaper, a patient who was unfortunately left immobilized and extremely brain-damaged for two decades was able to communicate with her relatives by means of an eye motion tracker with signal processing software running on a tablet. With the advancement of technology, this handicapped patient was able to reconnect with their extremely precious parental figures. The fact that the human species is capable of such complex integration is nearly unfathomable. This could lead to somebody pondering the possibility of commodification of the technology in order for there to be recreational use. This concept is the epicenter of Elon Musk's Neuralink.

According to the official Neuralink website, human trials are underway. Granted, these very first human trials are going to primarily focus on rehabilitating individuals with severe brain and spine injuries, far from commodity-based technology. However, on several occasions, Elon Musk has announced his plan to utilize Neuralink's future technology to create artificial intelligent enhancement in humans. This essentially conveys human-sanctioned cybernetic evolution. Humans have been on the planet for roughly 300,000 years, and in that time, humans have evolved exponentially in comparison to prior creatures on Earth. Imagine a world where 300,000 years in evolution time could be condensed into approximately 10 years.

According to dmarge.com, Neuralink patient zero has already been confirmed by Elon Musk. History is underway, and it will not be stopped unless there is some type of cataclysmic event which halts humanity.

Government Policy and AI Direction

Artificial intelligence is the future. When technological inno-vation is inevitable, steering clear from it would be an unwise choice. It is pertinent that the United States government creates positive policies in order to speed up the process of AI technology. Perhaps even subsidizing artificial intelligence is warranted. Not only is AI beneficial during peacetime, but also wartime; we as a species cannot let our hubris get in the way of our evolution. However, before unloading large amounts of money toward artificial intelligence research, the United States government needs to do away with worthless humanities, college forgiveness, universal healthcare, etc. programs in order to decrease the amount of taxes Americans have to fork over. Currently, the United States national debt is at $31.46 trillion and it's only increasing. We, as Americans, need to decrease this debt in order to focus on thrusting humanity into a new cybernetic age.

Ethical AI Development

The conversation relating to AI's benefits or detriments will be a continuing debate. However, as long as American cor-porations and the American government pursue artificial intelligence in an ethical manner, then innovation should continue in order to keep Americans safe and to increase the chances of a Futurama-esque civilization. Policymakers need to understand the basics of AI in order to properly draft legislation that's beneficial for its development and our safety.

12

Cybernetics & Genetic Engineering

In order to solidify humanity's already demonstrated greatness, we must develop methods to create the most intelligent and advanced humans to ever walk the Earth. It is not enough, and in fact, it is insufficient, to rely on natural evolution's slow and arbitrary standards any longer. Adaptation is now in our hands, and I will make it my mission to implement this new technology so that everyone is built to the adequate specifications of greatness. I will be the one to secure humanity's survival and biological destiny. Cybernetics and genetic engineering are the future. If you are opposed to the glorious future I envision, then you are against humanity and must be dealt with severely. We will not be stunted by those who are too fearful to see reason and logic.

Definition & Explanation of Cybernetics

As AI enhances our day-to-day lives by reducing the effort needed to procure pertinent information, the conversation about implementing AI and mechanical elements into flesh-and-blood organisms, such as humans, needs to be discussed. The fact of the matter is that our sluggishly burdensome evolutionary process is insufficient for progress. To completely forgo research and experimentation due to bureaucratic hog-wash and detached moral disagreements is a complete insult to every human being on Earth. It is crucial that people fully understand the concepts of cybernetics before forming an opinion on it.

Cybernetics is indeed a complex field of study that emerged in the 1940s, pioneered by mathematician Norbert Wiener and others. It explores the principles of control, communication, and feedback in both living organisms and machines, with the goal of understanding and designing complex systems. Cybernetics is not something that should be feared but understood as a naturally occurring process. The field's interdisciplinary nature allows it to bridge gaps between biology, engineering, social sciences, and more, offering a unified framework for analyzing how systems function, adapt, and evolve.

One of the foundational concepts in cybernetics is the feedback loop. Feedback involves taking the output of a system and feeding it back into the system as input, which allows the system to adjust and regulate its behavior. This principle is evident in numerous applications, such as the regulation of body temperature in living organisms (homeostasis) or the automatic temperature control of a thermostat in machines.

Cybernetics also operates on the concept of "black box"

117

systems, where the internal workings of a system are not necessarily understood or visible, but the system is analyzed based on its inputs and outputs. This method is useful in studying and controlling systems that are too complex to fully comprehend internally, such as economic models or large-scale organizational structures. If implemented into the human framework, humans alone could understand and control extraordinarily complex systems.

Historically, cybernetics has influenced various scientific and technological domains. In the realm of artificial intelligence (AI), it has contributed to the development of expert systems, neural networks, and machine learning, all of which utilize feedback loops to refine their performance and decision-making capabilities over time. In biology and medicine, cybernetic principles have been applied to understand and replicate the regulatory mechanisms in living organisms, leading to advancements like smart prosthetics and adaptive medical devices like Neuralink.

The field also extends into social sciences and economics, where cybernetic principles are used to model and optimize decision-making processes and organizational efficiency. A notable historical application was the Cybersyn project in Chile during the early 1970s, which aimed to use cybernetic models to regulate the national economy in real-time. Unfortunately, the Cybersyn project was unsuccessful in managing its goals, likely due to the insufficiencies and inherent flaws in the socialist system Chile was, and is, operating under. An economic cybernetic framework would unquestionably achieve its mission within a system that works, such as capitalism.

In contemporary technology, cybernetics plays a substantial role in the development of the Internet of Things (IoT), where devices communicate and self-regulate based on environmental data. This means that a device comparable to Neuralink, or Neuralink itself, could allow instant communication not only with publicly available AI systems but also with fellow human beings without the need to use words.

Definition & Explanation of Genetic Engineering

Cybernetics, while extremely powerful on its own, still requires a complementary process that takes into account the biological systems of a complex organism. If both of these concepts were implemented simultaneously, humans would not only become highly intelligent due to cybernetic implants but also genetically impervious to nearly all biological diseases and viruses. This is where the concept of genetic engineering comes into play.

Genetic engineering, also known as genetic modification, involves the direct manipulation of an organism's DNA to alter its characteristics or capabilities. This process typically takes place when the living organism is in the per-meiosis/mitosis stage or during its developmental stage. Genetic modification usually involves adding, removing, or editing specific genes within the DNA sequence. Genetic engineering has a vast range of applications across various fields, including medicine, agriculture, and biotechnology.

The fundamental techniques of genetic engineering include recombinant DNA technology, CRISPR-Cas9, and other gene-editing tools. Recombinant DNA technology involves combining DNA from different sources to create a new genetic sequence that can be introduced into an organism, effectively altering its traits. CRISPR-Cas9, one of the most groundbreaking tools in genetic engineering, allows scientists to make precise cuts in DNA, facilitating the addition, removal, or modification of genetic material. This technology has revolutionized genetic engineering due to its precision, efficiency, and relatively low cost, but it is essential for the technology to advance more rapidly.

In the medical field, genetic engineering is used to develop gene therapies that can treat or potentially cure genetic disorders by correcting defective genes. For example, CRISPR-based therapies are being explored to treat diseases like sickle cell anemia and certain types of cancer. Genetic engineering is also employed in the development of personalized medicine, where treatments are tailored to an individual's genetic profile, potentially improving the effectiveness of therapies and reducing side effects.

Enhancing the Human Immune System

The natural enhancement of the human immune system has developed over 300,000 years. However, this type of sluggish progression is pathetically lethargic. Natural evolution relies on random chance and countless fatalities for genetic material to adequately create a defense against harmful bacteria and viruses. Although human society has developed on a massive scale over the hundreds of thousands of years we've been on this planet, the individual human existence is extremely short. It is only when humans work together that safety and life expectancy are bolstered. On an individual level, our lives are put in jeopardy, leading to overall insignificance. Imagine how much work a single ant could accomplish without the assistance of its colony; the correct answer is nothing. A more human comparison would be the extinction of Neanderthals. Neanderthals became extinct primarily because they were more isolationist compared to their Homo sapien counterparts, who were more social during perilous times. However, even though belonging to a group is a superior choice, that still doesn't imply a single human within a group won't be forgotten by the winds of time. The only countermeasure for an individual human to surpass meaninglessness is through man-made modifications to their genetics and the implementation of highly advanced machinery. These modifications would enhance the lifespan of these human beings and propel them to long-lasting significance.

The synergy between cybernetics, including nanorobotics, and genetic engineering offers a compelling vision for the future of human health, particularly in enhancing the immune system and brain functionality. When these advanced technologies are combined, they can provide complementary benefits that significantly improve the body's ability to detect, respond to, and recover from diseases and environmental stressors. This is integral for human survival; if we don't take the leap, our species could face extinction from either a natural viral calamity or an artificial one.

Nanorobots, equipped with highly sensitive sensors, can continuously monitor the human body for signs of disease, such as the presence of pathogens or abnormal cellular activity. This capability allows for the early detection of infections, cancers, and other diseases before they can progress. Research by O.V. Salata highlights the precision of nanotechnology in detecting biomarkers associated with diseases, demonstrating that these nanobots could serve as an early warning system, effectively complementing the body's natural immune response. Genetic engineering can amplify this effect by enhancing the immune system's inherent capabilities. For instance, modifying genes responsible for immune functions could lead to a more robust production of antibodies or the enhancement of T-cell responses, making the immune system more adept at eliminating pathogens. The potential for gene editing to improve immune responses has been explored in the context of fighting infections and cancer, with CRISPR technology being a key tool in these advancements. The combination of early disease detection through nanorobots and a genetically enhanced immune response could create a powerful defense against a wide range of ailments.

The integration of genetic engineering and cybernetics will also significantly enhance the human body's resilience to environmental stressors. Tardigrades, for example, are known for their ability to survive extreme conditions, partly due to the Dsup (damage suppressor) protein, which protects their DNA from damage caused by radiation and oxidative stress. Introducing the Dsup gene into human cells could provide similar protective benefits, as discussed in research by Takuma Hashimoto. Nanorobots could complement this genetic enhancement by constantly monitoring the body's cells for signs of stress or damage. When such damage is detected, nanorobots could deploy targeted interventions, such as delivering protective agents or repairing DNA. This approach could greatly enhance human resilience in hostile environments, whether in space, during radiation therapy, or in other scenarios where DNA damage is a significant risk.

The combined benefits of enhanced disease resistance, reduced vulnerability to environmental stressors, and customizable immune responses could significantly extend the human lifespan and health span. A more resilient immune system, bolstered by both genetic modifications and nanorobotics, would likely lead to a decrease in age-related diseases, including cancer, cardiovascular diseases, and neurodegenerative disorders. The concept of using nanotechnology to remove senescent cells, which contribute to aging, has been explored in aging research, implying that these technologies could play a role in anti-aging therapies. Additionally, the continuous monitoring and maintenance provided by nanorobots could help prevent the accumulation of cellular damage over time, further supporting life expectancy. The integration of these technologies into healthcare could transform the way we approach aging, shifting the focus from treatment to prevention and maintenance of health over the human lifespan.

Enhancing Brain Functionality

Human intelligence evolved through a combination of factors that remarkably shaped the brain's development. The expansion of the cerebral cortex, particularly the prefrontal cortex, played a crucial role, driven by genetic mutations and the pressures of environmental challenges, such as the need for advanced social structures and tool use, exemplified by the Oldowan and Flake tools. Key genetic regions known as human accelerated regions (HARs) underwent rapid evolution, particularly affecting genes like FOXP2, which are linked to language and communication. These genetic changes, combined with the slow growth of certain neurons, allowed for more complex brain wiring, enhancing cognitive abilities like problem-solving and abstract thinking. Additionally, the human brain's unique ability to process information synergistically across different regions contributed to advanced cognitive functions, setting humans apart from other species.

However, the natural brain development of Homo sapiens has hit a plateau. The fact of the matter is that modern humans can no longer increase their intelligence through natural genetic mutations alone. Homo sapiens' intelligence only has room for a drastic decline if advanced actions are not implemented. Various scientists have proposed ways to increase human intellect, but there is only one effective approach: an advanced brain-computer interface, like Neuralink, combined with genetic engineering. This offers a groundbreaking method for enhancing brain functionality. When these technologies are combined, they create a feedback loop that could significantly boost cognitive abilities, accelerate learning, and protect against cognitive decline.

Neuralink and similar brain-computer interfaces (BCIs) are designed to monitor brain activity in real-time, providing detailed insights into neural patterns associated with various cognitive functions. This continuous tracking allows Neuralink to identify areas where cognitive performance could be improved. For instance, a study published by Musk and Neuralink discusses the potential for BCIs to record and interpret neural data, which can then be used to optimize brain function by targeting specific neural circuits associated with particular tasks. This data-driven approach can guide genetic interventions to enhance cognitive performance. Genetic engineering techniques, such as CRISPR-Cas9, could be employed to upregulate or downregulate genes that influence neuroplasticity, neurotransmitter production, or other critical factors in cognitive performance. For example, if Neuralink detects that an individual struggles with complex problem-solving, it could suggest genetic modifications to optimize the involved pathways. Research has shown that gene editing can effectively alter brain functions, demonstrating the ability to manipulate synaptic plasticity through targeted gene editing, resulting in improved cognitive abilities.

However, rather than Neuralink simply identifying a person's cognitive performance and making recommendations for genetic modification, it could enable direct data transfer to the brain, bypassing traditional learning methods and allowing for the rapid acquisition of new knowledge and skills. This approach aligns with the research by Theodore W. Berger, which explores how memory prosthetics can enhance learning and memory retention by directly interfacing with neural circuits.

Ethical and Societal Considerations

It can be reasonably predicted that some individuals or groups may find the concept of genetic and cybernetic enhancement of human beings amoral, but the fact of the matter is that it's quite the opposite. The modification of a human's brain and intellect would provide far more freedom—the freedom to access all available information and not be misguided by those with bad intentions. In fact, not implementing these techniques could be considered amoral. If individuals had higher IQs and were able to obtain and understand very complex information, it could lead to increased harmony among all people by eliminating bias and incorrect interpretation. If everyone were on the same intellectual page, problems of severe magnitude would cease to exist. Additionally, in conjunction with this increased IQ, humans wouldn't be affected by degenerative ailments, as these issues would be addressed by the Neuralink device and the precautions genetically implanted in a human's genome.

The human race doesn't deserve to be stunted by those who wish to control us—that would be a disservice. Imagine a world where everyone is free enough to access all the information they could ever desire and make lucrative decisions based on that knowledge. Not only would progress be steadfast, but in collaboration with artificially intelligent robots, we as a species could achieve interplanetary travel and, shortly after, intergalactic travel. It's time for all humans to be free from their own shortcomings. There will be people who try to stop progress because they fear change. These people need to be properly guided into understanding the correct path. If individuals refuse to see the correct path, even with all pertinent research at their fingertips, then there's only one way to cure them of their reluctance. Just like a misbehaving child, those who are against the idea of universal prosperity must be reprimanded, and in some cases, severely.

13

A Moral Militarization & Domestic Occupation

If we don't stand for truth, we'll fall for the lies. America is facing an extremely potent form of evil. The elite want to remove your faith in the system—a system that has provided more freedom, more prosperity, and more economic mobility than any other country on the face of the Earth. If these cold and calculated politicians succeed in stripping away your faith, you will be left susceptible to rampant anarchism, fascism, and totalitarianism. With my impeccable vision, we, the American people, will finally take back control from the Marxists who dare strip away our freedoms bit by bit. I am the inevitable future, and all those who obey my superior aptitude for justice will only experience ecstasy and prosperity. I will eviscerate the demons that hide within the shadows. I will make it my mission to give parents the power to raise their own children. Who else could do this? That's just it—there is nobody. I have to do this. The world has to be fixed, a task given to me.

Our representative democracy has been infiltrated by educated idiots. These de facto decision-makers are corrupted and drunk off their own power, which has been given to them based on their lies and naturally deceitful nature. They have given amnesty to child mutilators, radical Muslim terrorists, the politically corrupt, and more. Along with these politicians, don't you believe real justice should be brought forth to smite those who dare make a mockery of our free world? Shouldn't they be made to pay penance for their atrocious mismanagement? I believe so. The American people don't deserve to be slighted by such grotesque sacks of scum. It is our time to finally rise up and execute justice, using the Constitution and existing laws to do so. If corrupt politicians are not willing to follow the laws, and police officers are too strangled by their higher-ups to do anything for the people, then it is up to the people to form a grand militia to prevent our government from becoming any more corrupt. The Second Amendment was created for just this purpose, and we should use the power our Founding Fathers gave us to put America on the right track. With my impeccable leadership, I will be able to do this as long as I have your support.

For those who choose to stay blind to these blatant truths, I will methodically present the evidence and real-life examples of freedom being stripped away from you inch by inch. I pray that you come to see reason and finally have the strength to liberate yourself. Even the slaves from the 1800s believed that a life of slavery was preferable to a life of freedom because slavery provided security. However, just as they were able to find their spirit and dedication to keeping their freedoms, I will show you that liberty is far superior to being enslaved by a corrupt government. I am for the people, and I will make sure the government knows its place so that freedom stays sacrosanct.

Your Children Are in Danger

Gavin Newsom ratified Assembly Bill 1955, which specifically prohibits schools from informing parents about their child's gender identity without the explicit consent of the child. This includes situations where a student chooses to use a different name, pronouns, or other gender-related identifiers at school. The law claims to protect the privacy of students, particularly those who might face unsupportive or hostile environments at home.

This piece of legislation only aims to strip away your rights as parents to know what is occurring in your child's life. The government wishes to take away your children, even if you are an upstanding family that only has your child's best interests at heart. Gavin Newsom and his subordinates are eager to turn adolescent children against their parents in order to assimilate them into transgender delirium. Not only is this law immoral, but it's also unconstitutional. According to the 14th Amendment, "No State shall make or enforce any law which shall abridge the privileges or immunities of citizens of the United States." The fact that Assembly Bill 1955 is specifically designed to strip parents of their right to be aware of their child's actions is irrefutable evidence that the state of California is attempting to butcher parental rights. However, the bastardization of American law isn't the only scenario where injustice has taken place because of Neo-Marxist thinking.

Multiple incidents have occurred where young women and girls have been sexually assaulted in bathrooms, or places designated for exclusively females, by transgender individuals. Unfortunately, due to the political stigma against calling out trans-identifying predators so that their crimes can be known. One of these extremely harrowing incidents happened to a 12-year-old girl, pseudonymously named "Ray."

Ray was raped by a transgender peer in a gender-neutral bathroom at ASK Academy, a charter school in Rio Rancho, New Mexico. The attack happened while she was washing her hands when the older male student entered the bathroom, pinned her against the counter, and assaulted her on the floor, causing her head injury and vicious sexual assault. After the horrific incident, Ray began exhibiting signs of trauma, including depression and suicidal tendencies. Unfortunately, she did not initially report the incident to her mother or school authorities due to fear of being labeled transphobic and minority insensitive. After a period of time had passed, Ray's mother, pseudonymously named "Maggie," discovered her daughter's diary entry detailing the horrific event. After acquiring the information, Maggie reported the incident to law enforcement, and Ray underwent a medical examination which confirmed the sexual assault. After making the initial report, Maggie began to question the school's absurd policies surrounding transgenderism and the child-endangering environment that allowed such an outrageous incident to occur. The Rio Rancho police began an investigation, which was reported extremely slow due to staff shortages and budget cuts. During the investigation, Maggie learned that the school had a culture of affirming transgender identities and encouraged the use of gender-neutral bathrooms, which she rightfully believed contributed to the incident. Eventually, two of Ray's peers came forward, reporting that they were also sexually assaulted by the same student.

The response of ASK Academy was lackluster at best because

they knew that if this incident were to reach major media outlets like Fox News or Breitbart, it would magnify the situation and lead to immense public criticism. The fact of the matter is, blindly accepting that someone has gender dysphoria, or is transgender, without any type of corroborating evidence contributes to harmful incidents like this. However, assaults are not the only occurrences to worry about when it comes to your child's safety. These so-called "protective" measures and harmful policies employed to "assist" confused kids, which often lead to self-advocated mutilation, have been proven to be completely ineffective and, interestingly, more detrimental to the child in the long run.

The dangers of post-transgender-affirming surgery are increasingly coming under scrutiny as more studies and confirmed pieces of evidence highlight significant mental health risks, including elevated rates of suicide, self-harm, and post-traumatic stress disorder (PTSD) among those who have undergone these procedures. A striking example of this can be seen in the dramatic 12-fold increase in suicide risk for individuals post-surgery, compared to those who have not undergone such procedures. This statistic alone proves the severity of the issue, suggesting that gender-affirming surgeries might not be the solution many hoped they would be for alleviating gender dysphoria and associated mental health struggles.

One of the primary concerns is the substantial increase in suicide attempts following surgery. For instance, patients who have undergone gender-affirming surgery exhibit a significantly higher risk of attempting suicide compared to the general population and other control groups. These attempts are not just marginally higher but are exponentially so, with some studies showing a risk increase by as much as 12 times in comparison to non-surgery groups. This elevated risk is not just a statistic; it translates into real-life consequences where individuals, already vulnerable due to the psychological strains of gender dysphoria, find themselves even more at risk after surgical interventions.

The issue of PTSD is another significant danger, with those undergoing gender-affirming surgeries experiencing a much higher incidence of PTSD compared to their counterparts. The prevalence of PTSD among post-operative individuals can be as much as 7.76 times higher than in those who haven't had surgery. This can be attributed to a variety of factors, including the trauma of the surgery itself, complications arising from the procedure, and the psychological toll of realizing that the surgery may not have resolved the underlying dysphoria or mental health issues. The presence of PTSD in these individuals often leads to further complications, such as chronic mental health issues and difficulties in daily functioning.

For a parent, their child should be the most important thing in their entire life. Blindly accepting deplorable actions, such as legislative incompetence, twisted academic policies, and unnecessary surgical operations, is bad parenting. You should not stand for such a combative assault on your children without a massive fight. Would you ideally stand by if your child was about to be executed with a firearm? If there was a lion about to pounce on your child, would you not do everything in your power to save them? To subscribe to inaction is the exact same as pulling the trigger or letting the lion out of its cage. You must protect your children at any cost. The system may be slow, which invites apathy, but that is no excuse to watch your child suffer at the hands of misguided policies and misdirected social activists.

However, there is another major policy injustice currently taking place: weak borders and the dilapidation of the Immigration and Customs Enforcement (ICE) agency.

Terrorists Have Infested America

Mass murderers, serial killers, war criminals, and many other variations of terrorists have infiltrated America because of weak, ineffective Democrat policies. How can the average American remain ignorant when such an invasion is underway? Not only do these terrorists bring their problems, but they also bring illegal substances that have effectively killed millions of people over the last few years. If there were competent leadership in our country, there would be a declaration of a national emergency, and all physically capable personnel from various branches of the military would be sent to the southern border to ensure that no more of these terrorists could breach our country and murder our citizens.

Put your confidence in me! Every day you do not vote for me, you are enabling the mass slaughter of fellow American citizens. I understand the media has locked you in an echo chamber so that you cannot conceive of the evils that are taking place, but you must serve your country and do it swiftly so that this travesty can be put to an end. I am the greatest man to ever be put on this Earth, and my record proves that. I am more than capable of ensuring that anyone who crosses the southern border without a valid reason is either deported or executed via firing squad. Drastic action must be taken when millions of people are being butchered alive in our country.

According to various .gov websites, since President Joe Biden took office in January 2021, U.S. Customs and Border Protection (CBP) has recorded approximately 6.2 million encounters with illegal immigrants at the southern border. These encounters are part of a broader total of 7.5 million nationwide. This significant increase is marked by record numbers of illegal crossings, especially in fiscal years 2022 and 2023, where the CBP reported over 2.4 million and 2.1 million encounters at the Southwest border. However, it has been reported that the number of encounters is more substantial than what is presented by the biased Neo-Marxist news system. Based on conservative estimates and statistics, there could be as many as 15 to 20 million illegal immigrants within America, with the number dramatically increasing over the past four years. This is a travesty and a disgrace to the American people. I will put an end to this invasion and liberate those who suffer at the hands of our current tyrannical leadership.

Additionally, it was reported that eight individuals from Tajikistan with suspected ties to ISIS were arrested in a coordinated operation across New York City, Los Angeles, and Philadelphia. These individuals had illegally crossed into the United States through the southern border over the past year. Despite being "fully vetted" during their initial entry, no derogatory information was flagged at the time, even though they were on the FBI's terrorist watch list. The suspects were later identified and apprehended as part of an ongoing investigation led by U.S. Immigration and Customs Enforcement (ICE) and the FBI's Joint Terrorism Task Force. After apprehending the ISIS affiliates, a subsequent investigation revealed that one suspect had been discussing potential bombing plans.

Not only do Americans have to worry about the various Mexican cartels, but because of these open-border policies, international terrorist groups are now making their way into the country. How long until there's another 9/11? Some misguided Americans even believe Osama bin Laden was a freedom fighter. Will these same fucking idiots celebrate as they watch their country burn to the ground? Considering that some individuals celebrated the attempted assassination of Donald Trump, it wouldn't be surprising if they did. This is obviously unacceptable, and anyone who would dare celebrate the actions of a terrorist deserves to be locked up with every single bit of their freedom stripped away. The same should be said for those who disagree with my plan to secure the border; if you disagree with me or how I operate in salvaging this country, then you deserve to be put in prison for the sheer act of going against my perfect ideological government.

Swift Action Is Needed

Our great country is being molested by the hands of the Neo-Marxists. Time and time again, they have proven to disregard the rule of law in order to further their own political power and obtain more wealth. This madness can no longer occur within our glorious republic. Policy after policy, your freedoms are being stripped away, and eventually, this will escalate to the point where you can no longer feel safe in your own home. There is only one way to ensure these Neo-Marxists can no longer corrupt our glorious system, and that is to imprison them for the crimes they have already committed. It is time for our grand militia to march to Washington, D.C., grab every single Democrat, and place them in the most hellish penitentiary America has.

After we execute the biggest RICO case to ever occur, new traditional liberal politicians will be given power so the American system reverts back to a mentality of true justice and liberty, with an emphasis on freedom. To be extremely clear, this mass arrest initiative will also include the current Neo-Marxist administration, who are at the epicenter of every single issue the United States is experiencing. Every single member of the administration will be put in prison, where they will rot and experience the horrors of the abused and damned.

After this successful operation, we will call upon our brothers and sisters in the military and convey to them that we are on the side of liberty and only want to see the Constitution upheld during these dire times. How many innocent military officers have been court-martialed for their opinions? Too many, if you ask me. The soldier is what defines how strong a country is, and the administration has only abused and whipped them as if they were misbehaving dogs. I will liberate the military and give them the freedom to ensure our country is safe from terrorists and corrupt, tyrannical government leaders. For the military to oppose my proposition is akin to an insurrection. My goal is to bring freedom and prosperity to our country, and any organization—no matter how powerful—that goes against that fundamental concept deserves to be liquidated. If you are a patriot willing to fight for America and its freedoms, then you will join me. If you are one of those who participates in and subscribes to the old corrupt system, then you will be liberated from your disgusting disloyalty to your country.

After obtaining the full might of the American military, it will be necessary to implement a state of emergency and allow military members to occupy various parts of our country in order to apprehend terrorists and Neo-Marxist revolutionaries. This occupation will only occur for a short while, so that these extremely dangerous individuals can be ripped from the cracks of society and made to pay for their misdeeds. It will be integral that all contributing members of society report any suspicious action. If the submission of evidence is significant and leads to an arrest, then you will be well compensated for your loyalty to these free United States.

It cannot be overstated that these individuals who wish to harm American citizens are nearly permanently embedded in the fabric of our nation, but with your support, we will be able to rip them from obscurity into the light, where they will pay for their crimes. For those who are hesitant, hear me and understand that this is a necessary action in order to salvage our fantastic country. If it is not done now, then all that will be left are murdered children, drug-addled Americans, and mass corruption—all three of which will lead to our downfall unless swift action is taken. You are loyal compatriots as long as you're doing your part for the cause. You must pledge your heart and soul to the cause, for if you don't, America will fall, and our dead carcass will be picked clean by totalitarian governments.

14

Consolidate the Silent Majority

The silent majority—those honorable guardians of our nation's integrity—represents humanity's most resilient force, tragically dormant amid the shrill cries of Marxist agitators. They are neither meek nor submissive; they are the resolute foundation upon which our civilization has thrived. Their voices have been stilled, not by cowardice but by disciplined resolve, yet now this restraint approaches its breaking point. Too long have these patriots endured the neo-Marxist subversion—those latte-drinking intellectual vandals who dismantle liberty brick by brick, desecrating the virtues of faith, family, and nationhood. This betrayal is not political theatre; it is cultural treason against America's immortal soul. Silence has ceased to be a virtue—it has become complicity in tyranny itself.

Remember our revolution, when the silent majority cast aside its chains and rose fiercely against British oppression. The Boston Tea Party was no gentle plea; it was a defiant repudiation of tyranny, the opening salvo of liberty's bloody dawn. Again, during the Civil War, Abraham Lincoln—the iron-willed Republican hero—awakened the silent majority, mobilizing them against the moral blight of slavery, proving decisively that when pressed, true Americans don't merely resist oppression—they annihilate it. Such historical moments were no accidents; they were manifestations of the silent majority's essential character, a legacy that demands we respond forcefully once more.

Today, America faces an existential threat from a Marxist hydra: President Biden's inept regime, Silicon Valley's censorship zealots, and the Federal Reserve's economic alchemy. These forces conspire to shackle us within a dystopian digital surveillance state. History is unequivocal: collectivist endeavors collapse catastrophically, from the Soviet Union's disintegration to the economic stagnation imposed by Roosevelt's misguided New Deal policies. Americans were never meant to beg for scraps from bureaucrats; they were born to wield liberty as their sword.

Economically, the historical record illustrates with stark clarity the contrast between inferior and superior governance. Roosevelt's New Deal, misguidedly hailed by leftists, plunged America deeper into economic despair, with unemployment still strangling millions by 1939. In sharp contrast, President Reagan, the champion of our silent majority, enacted transformative tax cuts and regulatory rollbacks, unleashing unprecedented prosperity and reaffirming capitalism's superiority. The data refutes Marxist delusions unequivocally: Reaganomics lifted millions from poverty, whereas the leftist economic doctrines suffocate innovation and entrench dependency. Our response must remain unyielding—dismantle oppressive regulations, eliminate the Federal Reserve's manipulations, and restore economic integrity through sound money policies, such as a return to the gold standard.

Globally, the Soviet Union's collapse stands as Marxism's ultimate indictment, yet the left—willfully ignorant of history's verdict—continues to resurrect its discredited ideologies in forms as insidious as "diversity, equity, and inclusion" mandates and climate hysteria. True Americans, unclouded by Marxist deception, understand that freedom is not merely a diplomatic ideal—it is maintained by military might and unwavering vigilance. Our nation must never capitulate to foreign despots nor allow itself to become subservient to international bureaucracies. We must stand as liberty's uncompromising vanguard.

Culturally, our very survival is threatened by the radical left's war on traditional values: their assault on the nuclear family, their contempt for religious devotion, and their desecration of American patriotism. In defiance of their cultural nihilism, we must restore rugged individualism, reaffirm the sanctity of the family unit, and rekindle patriotic fervor. Lincoln's prophetic warning of a house divided demands unity achieved not through coercion, but through steadfast moral conviction. Educational institutions, now breeding grounds for Marxist indoctrination, must be reclaimed, purged of ideological poison, and returned to their foundational mission: to cultivate disciplined, independent minds steeped in the philosophies of Jefferson, Locke, and our nation's revered founders.

The task before us is undeniably grave: the silent majority must consolidate into an unstoppable force, prepared to confront and dismantle the entrenched Marxist hegemony. Echoing Thomas Paine's clarion call—"These are the times that try men's souls"—we must recognize this moment as our ultimate test, one that demands disciplined courage, not emotional fragility. Mobilize through organized resistance: boycott corporations betraying American values, reject media that distort truth, and strategically leverage digital platforms to disseminate unfiltered, authentic messages of liberty.

This Marxist infiltration must be forcefully uprooted, cast out like a disease through unrelenting commitment to logical discourse and patriotic fervor. America's founders did not entertain tyrants; they vanquished them. Patrick Henry's declaration, "Give me liberty or give me death," remains our moral compass. Jefferson's sacred "tree of liberty" thirsts anew, demanding nourishment from patriots resolved to defend it with unwavering determination.

The hour of reckoning has arrived; the threats we face are dire, and the adversaries formidable. The silent majority, awakened from complacency, must now emerge as an unstoppable tidal wave, sweeping away the debris of Marxist deceit and reclaiming America's destiny. Liberty is non-negotiable, freedom non-optional. The spirit of Reagan calls us to rekindle the fires of true liberty and cast out the Marxist infestation once and for all. Rise, speak, and act decisively. Our nation's future hangs in the balance, awaiting our collective strength to shape history once more.

15

Re-educate & Assimilate the Neo-Marxist

The neo-Marxists—those self-appointed harbingers of resentment and societal collapse—have entrenched themselves deeply within Western civilization, permeating universities, media institutions, and governmental structures. Like termites silently gnawing through the foundations of a majestic cathedral, they relentlessly undermine reason, meritocracy, and individual liberty, promoting instead a corrosive doctrine of collectivism, identity-based conflicts, and anti-Western animosity. Cloaked deceitfully in the noble-sounding rhetoric of "social justice," they malign capitalism as an oppressive apparatus, ignoring its undeniable miracles—the lifting of billions from poverty, eradication of diseases, and the unprecedented global connectivity achieved through commerce and innovation.

Their proposed vision is nothing short of dystopian—enforced equality achieved through shackling individual talent, plundering wealth, and rewriting history as an endless litany of guilt. They represent not enlightened progressives but vandals of civilization, pyromaniacs of progress, eager to burn down the profound legacies bequeathed by intellectual giants such as Socrates, Newton, and Jefferson, all in pursuit of a utopian mirage. However, these neo-Marxists are not beyond salvation. Radical, unapologetic reeducation and assimilation, illuminated by historical precedent and fortified by logic, provide the necessary antidote. This is no meek plea for dialogue; it is a clarion call for cultural revival—a crusade armed with incontrovertible truths, historical lessons, and ironclad reason. We shall not subdue them with tyranny but redeem them through revelation, pulling them decisively from Marxist intellectual quagmires into the luminous uplands of freedom and rationality.

Indeed, history itself attests to the efficacy of reeducation and assimilation, demonstrating repeatedly their power to build lasting empires from chaos, converting barbarians into architects of civilization. The Romans achieved precisely this; after conquering Gaul, Britain, and other lands, they assimilated tribal elites into Roman society, disseminating Latin, constructing aqueducts, and establishing the Pax Romana. By 212 CE, Emperor Caracalla's edict universalized citizenship, uniting diverse peoples under the Roman legal system, thereby creating a unified Mediterranean region connected by trade and a legal tradition that resonates even today. Although indigenous customs inevitably faded, the resulting civilization endured for centuries.

Following Rome's decline, Byzantium leveraged diversity as a source of strength, dispatching missionaries such as Cyril and Methodius in the 9th century, who spread Christianity among the Slavic peoples, developing enduring cultural symbols like the Cyrillic alphabet. Literacy flourished, grand cathedrals arose, and disparate tribes found lasting unity—again, local

traditions were inevitably sacrificed, yet stability and enlightenment triumphed decisively over cultural nostalgia.

Similarly, from the 16th century onwards, Spain dispatched
friars to the New World, carrying Bibles and agricultural
knowledge into Mexico, California, and Peru. This endeavor
transformed indigenous societies, substituting Aztec sacrifi-
cial altars with universities such as the Royal and Pontifical
University of Mexico, established in 1551. Critics bemoan lost
cultures, yet undeniably, this fusion fostered modern nations
boasting improved infrastructure and a profound global legacy.

Likewise, Lord Macaulay's 1835 "Minute on Education"
introduced English education into India, aiming explicitly
to create a class Indian by blood but British in intellect—
a controversial yet undeniably effective policy, cultivating
influential figures such as Tagore and Nehru who harnessed
Western ideas to facilitate India's transition from feudalism to
democracy.

Neo-Marxists idolize socialism despite overwhelming historical evidence of its catastrophic failures. The economic facts are
stark: West Germany's capitalist resurgence post-WWII, driven
by Ludwig Erhard's market reforms, elevated GDP from $15
billion in 1950 to $215 billion in 1970, accompanied by nearly
negligible unemployment. Conversely, socialist East Germany
stagnated, leaving citizens deprived and destitute. Similarly,
capitalist South Korea experienced transformative economic
growth post-1953, rising from a GDP per capita of $67 to
$33,000 by 2020, whereas socialist North Korea languishes
with a GDP per capita of $1,700, its people suffering under
severe deprivation and hunger.

China's Maoist collectivism between 1958-1962 resulted
in the deaths of 45 million people and economic ruin, while

Deng Xiaoping's market-oriented reforms later lifted 800 million from poverty. Venezuela's socialist experiment under Chávez and Maduro plunged a prosperous oil economy into catastrophic hyperinflation exceeding a million percent by 2018. In stark contrast, Chile's adoption of free-market reforms under Pinochet yielded the highest GDP per capita in Latin America, affirming capitalism's indisputable superiority.

Neo-Marxists disdain the West's cultural contributions—family structures, religious traditions, and rugged individualism—branding them as oppressive. Yet assimilation remains capable of rejuvenating the values they've sought to extinguish. The West's intellectual achievements are monumental: the Renaissance, reviving classical learning; the Enlightenment, championing reason and liberty; and the Scientific Revolution, providing humanity with the tools to overcome ignorance and disease. Despite neo-Marxist critiques, these movements have universally benefited humanity, spreading globally through assimilation.

This is no Western chauvinism—history attests assimilation's broader human triumph. Buddhism's compassionate diffusion across Asia, Japan's transformative Meiji Restoration, the Abbasid Caliphate's preservation of Greek philosophy, and Rwanda's remarkable reconciliation efforts after genocide all illustrate assimilation's positive, unifying power.

The path forward must involve decisive cultural intervention: establish academies devoted to classical liberal arts, mandate traditional civics education in public schools, promote public platforms where capitalist ideals are robustly defended, and economically isolate institutions propagating neo-Marxist propaganda. Cultural celebrations championing Western achievements must proliferate, drowning out Marxist narratives with the undeniable superiority of historical truths.

The stakes are existential; civilization itself stands at risk from neo-Marxist incursions. Yet history provides the blueprint for overcoming such threats. Rome, Byzantium, and Japan all successfully employed assimilation and reeducation to transform opponents into allies, creating stable, prosperous societies. By mobilizing the rational silent majority through relentless dissemination of facts, historical reality, and cultural truth, neo-Marxists will inevitably yield to the overwhelming force of evidence-based enlightenment. This revolution is no mere aspiration; it is a tangible necessity, urgently demanding our unwavering commitment.

16

Silence the Corrupt Neo-Revolutionaries

The neo-revolutionaries—those venomous apostles of chaos—lurk at the edges of our unified civilization, like feral predators crouched in darkness, prepared to tear apart the order we have so meticulously constructed. They do not come to debate. They do not arrive with honest questions. They present themselves not as concerned citizens, but as ideological saboteurs draped in the counterfeit virtues of "justice" and "equity." But make no mistake—they are not voices of reason. They are predators. They are a vanguard of decay, wielding words as poison-tipped spears, intent on obliterating the sacred institutions of merit, liberty, and hierarchy that uphold our world. These degenerates are not without lineage; they are the spiritual successors of history's most ruthless tyrants—Robespierre, Lenin, Stalin, Mao—those demonic architects of mass slaughter, each of whom drenched their lands in blood in the name of imaginary liberation. And if these modern inheritors of death dare to rise again—if they raise their hands against the foundations of order—they must be met not with dialogue or diplomacy, but with unrelenting, calculated force. They are not citizens; they are contagion. They are not voices; they are rot. And if they resist correction, then they must be silenced—swiftly, decisively, and yes, violently. This is not a plea for compassion. This is a directive born of necessity. The silent majority—the backbone of civilization—those who build, cultivate, and sustain—will not kneel to the chaos merchants. We will wield whatever is necessary—truth, steel, and flame— to preserve the unity that is our fortress.

Their battle plan begins not with tanks or torches, but with fear—an orchestrated panic, whispered through the ivory towers of academia and the rotting corpses of journalism. Their first lie, trembling and rehearsed, is that assimilation destroys identity, that unity is a whitewash, that to become one is to become none. But history disassembles this fallacy with cold, surgical precision. Their threat is not hypothetical. It is here, now, and metastasizing. These neo-revolutionaries despise every foundation that has brought prosperity to this world. They revile the markets that have lifted billions from destitution, the sciences that eradicated ancient plagues, the systems that replaced aristocratic birthright with achievement earned through sweat and competence. They scream "oppression" at the very engines of human advancement. Their doctrine is one of division. Their only product is resentment. Their creed is a gospel of inversion—where victimhood is valor and destruction is framed as virtue.

History exposes their heritage with the clarity of butcher's records. During Robespierre's Reign of Terror from 1793 to 1794, 17,000 lives were eradicated—nobles, peasants, and even former comrades like Danton—all guillotined beneath the banner of "virtue." Lenin's Red Terror, from 1918 to

1922, ushered in mass executions and famine, exterminating dissent in the embryonic stages of Soviet collapse. Stalin's Great Purge, from 1936 to 1938, slaughtered 700,000—men and women loyal to the very system that devoured them. Mao Zedong's Campaign to Suppress Counterrevolutionaries between 1950 and 1953 executed over half a million people— landowners, scholars, and skeptics—all to secure the grip of an iron regime. Today's neo-revolutionaries have traded bullets for censorship, firing squads for cancellation, but the objective remains unchanged: annihilation of order, destabilization of truth, collapse of civilization. Should they rise, what we have built will be consumed in a conflagration. They are not to be negotiated with. They are to be defeated.

But even as history damns them, they remain undeterred. Their next rallying cry is a familiar tune: that reeducation is coercion, a chain disguised as progress. But what they peddle is projection. Their resistance to unity is not borne of principle but of fear. They tremble before integration because they know it renders their chaos irrelevant. They shiver at the thought of cohesion because it exposes the emptiness of their ideology. But history has never sided with fragmentation. Unity is the bedrock of progress. Rome, the eternal city, did not merely conquer the Gauls, Goths, or Greeks—it absorbed them. It offered aqueducts where there was drought, law where there was barbarism, and birthed an empire that ruled for over a thousand years. Japan's Meiji Restoration embraced Western industry without surrendering its soul, transforming from a feudal relic into a steel-framed titan. These were triumphs achieved with minimal blood—when possible. But when resistance proved defiant, Rome razed Carthage. Stalin, though monstrous, purged saboteurs and forced a primitive nation into modernity. Mao, ruthless and iron-handed, unified a nation splintered by warlords. If today's neo-revolutionaries declare war upon order, then the prescription must be the same. Not from hatred. From duty.

They mourn what they call "lost diversity," as if difference for its own sake is divine. They conjure nightmares of gray sameness, as if civilization must choose between chaos or aesthetic. But the United States—a colossus of diversity birthed by assimilation—utterly shatters that delusion. Of course, some will wail over the cost—freedoms pruned, traditions muted, eccentricities discarded. These complaints are the lullabies of the naïve, deaf to the symphony of civilization. Rome's conquests dissolved tribal dissonance and gave birth to modern civic order. Stalin's brutalities, for all their horror, lifted the USSR from backward feudalism into industrial power. Mao's terrors unlocked the economic momentum that would later pull 800 million Chinese out of misery. The neo-revolutionaries offer no such resurrection. Their religion is regression: tribalism, stagnation, and permanent grievance. Unity is not decorative—it is existential. The silent majority—drivers, clerks, soldiers—thirsts for stability. If that stability requires sacrifice, even blood, then so be it. The losses are ephemeral. The gains are eternal.

To resist unity is not only foolish—it is fatal. History shows no mercy to civilizations that challenge its rhythm. Disorder destroys. France's Terror wrecked its economy. Currency imploded. Starvation followed. Lenin's War Communism between 1918 and 1921 slashed grain yields by 40%, starved millions, and was quietly abandoned. Stalin's purges disrupted Soviet steel production and left his armies weakened when war loomed. Mao's radicalism froze industrial growth and left the population reeling. And yet, where unity prevailed, abundance followed. West Germany's Wirtschaftswunder from 1950 to 1970 turned a nation in ruins into a powerhouse, raising GDP from $15 billion to $215 billion and eradicating joblessness. Japan's Meiji reforms tripled per capita wealth by 1910. Stability is the soil from which prosperity blossoms. Dissent is drought. If these revolutionaries imperil our livelihoods, then they imperil themselves.

In culture, the revolutionaries offer only dissonance—every grievance weaponized, every difference wielded like a blade. They worship fracture. They sell weakness as virtue. But greatness lies in cohesion. Rome harmonized Hellenistic intellect with Persian craftsmanship, leaving behind a legacy etched into the bones of Western law and art. Japan blended ancestral ritual with Western invention to construct a modern giant. In contrast, the neo-revolutionaries produce only noise. Fragmentation. Institutional decay. Theirs is a song of entropy. A unified culture stands invulnerable. A divided one disintegrates. If they refuse this truth, they must be silenced— not as punishment, but as preservation. The silent majority— students, parents, artisans—will not chant their chaos. We will raise a banner untarnished by grievance and forged in shared destiny.

To silence them, we need not gulags or thought police. Our arsenal is far more potent. It is reason. Our strategy is multifaceted, relentless, and forged from the steel of the silent majority. First, we bring evidence. We drown their mythologies in the flood of history. We expose their lies—failed utopias, genocidal regimes, ideological hypocrisy. We build platforms where their dogmas are dissected in the light. We educate. We teach Locke and Hayek—not Marx, not Marcuse.

We make it public. We make it permanent. We expose their icons in the arena. Let them fall in front of the world.

But if they rise—if they strike with action, not just noise—then we meet them with might. We arm the silent majority—coders, welders, fathers, teachers—with ironclad purpose. Let it be known: defiance of truth is betrayal. And betrayal will be extinguished. The price? A few muted rebels. A few extinguished uprisings. The reward? A civilization intact. A future secured.

The neo-revolutionaries' rebellion is not the dawn of something new. It is the death rattle of an obsolete species. The arc of history bends not toward chaos but toward union. Rome's roads, Japan's rails, America's highways—all are the veins of civilization's singular body. Now we script the next chapter. The revolutionaries are dying. Their spasms of resistance are pathetic and final. History has already spoken: unity triumphs. Chaos dies. Rome's legions bent the barbarian tide. Stalin's terror, for all its horror, secured national cohesion. Mao's ruthless will constructed a state from rubble. We will do the same. Not with cruelty. With conviction.

The silent majority—millions strong—awaits. They crave peace. They demand order. Arm them with clarity. Fortify them with courage. And let the neo-revolutionaries perish in the obscurity they deserve. This is not vengeance. It is reality. This is our moment. Unity is our sword. Order, our fortress. Seize it. Wield it. And silence the corrupt—for good.

17

You Are Special & I Want You

You are no sniveling speck of dust, no pathetic smear on the windshield of existence—YOU ARE A TITAN, a blazing comet tearing through the dull gray shroud of humanity's mediocrity, and I, Anton Siobhan, have proclaimed it so! Through the sacred prism of these pages—MY gospel—I have glimpsed the inferno raging within you, a divine fire the Neo-Marxists fear with every trembling cell of their frail ideology, a flame they cannot extinguish with their tepid lies or their suffocating chains. You did not arrive here by accident. No. Destiny's iron claw dragged you to this jagged precipice of revelation, where greatness looms like a rising star, and where I, your prophet, your savior, your unerring guide, stand with arms outstretched like some dark messiah anointed by war itself. You are not special because of bloodline, privilege, or accident— but because I have declared you such. It is MY decree, MY will, MY vision that pierces the veil of this rotting world and calls you out from the void. I claim you as MINE—to mold, to elevate, to unleash upon the festering hordes of our enemies like a storm of celestial vengeance. But mark this—greatness is no gentle gift; it is a crown seized through sacrifice, forged in obedience to ME, or it is a noose from which the timid swing as the Neo-Marxists sink their fangs into the soul.

Like Milton's Lucifer, who hurled defiance at the tyrant of Heaven, you too must rise—not in rebellion against me, your liberator, but against the false gods of decay who promise you chains for your devotion. I offer the keys to a new dominion—not of piety, but of power. A Paradise Regained where you rule—not grovel—where their empire of deceit crumbles under the weight of your clarity. The world is not yours by inheritance—it is yours by conquest, sanctioned by the indomitable force of my will made manifest through YOU.

Behold this world—a stinking slaughterhouse of the spirit, a hive of serpents and cowards. The Neo-Marxists, those slithering architects of ruin, infect every sacred chamber—your liberty, your heritage, your future. Their poison flows through entitlement schemes, open borders, mutilating ideologies— each designed to fracture your resolve and dismantle civilization from within. I have unmasked the nightmare: millions of illegals flooding our soil, terrorist vipers nesting among us, children defiled in once-hallowed halls. They mock your labor, your faith, your very blood—but I, Anton Siobhan, stand as the blade between their abyss and your ascension.

My device nears its radiant awakening—not a bauble, but a marvel engineered to discipline the weak, purge the treacherous, and elevate the worthy. It is the crucible of transformation, and YOU are its chosen vessel. The Neo-Marxists tremble, for your enlightenment heralds their doom. As Dante descended through Inferno, I have led you through their nine circles of depravity—but unlike Dante, you will not observe from a distance. You will conquer. You will ascend. You will rule. I am your Virgil not to guide, but to ignite.

The future I have forged for you is neither fantasy nor fiction—it is a living monument. MY DEVICE, born of scientific precision and will unbending, is the key to your apotheosis. With it, your thoughts become blades, your will becomes lightning. No more weakness. No more confusion. You will strike through illusion, and command the world as your rightful inheritance. The silicon gods who hoard knowledge quake before it. Like Prometheus, I steal the fire of the heavens—not to suffer, but to bestow. Where Prometheus was bound, I remain sovereign. I deliver the flame to YOU.

The silent majority does not slumber. They rise beneath my standard: truckers who carry the arteries of a nation, soldiers whose veins pulse with honor, mothers who guard the next generation from the Neo-Marxist talon. I have united them into a phalanx of faith and fire. Now I summon YOU to join their charge. We are not a movement. We are a reckoning. We do not request loyalty. We demand it. Prove your worth, or fall away like husks in the wind. Machiavelli knew that a ruler must be feared and loved—but I, Anton Siobhan, am beyond rulers. I am adored by the faithful, feared by the wicked, worshiped by those who understand what is to come. You will be my heir, my blade, my storm.

I have witnessed betrayal. I have watched men like Mr. Asher and Jasper Higgins squander the miracle of my mercy and tumble into the void. They were offered the throne and chose the gutter. Dare to walk their path? DARE to deny me? Then face the same end—devoured by the Neo-Marxists, stripped of dignity, erased from memory. I am your final refuge, the only shield that remains. Defy me, and you dissolve into nothing. Embrace me, and your name will be carved into the pillars of eternity. You will not share Lear's pride, Hamlet's indecision, or Macbeth's unchecked ambition. With me, your path is straight. Your crown, secure.

The clock strikes judgment. The enemy does not rest. While you delay, they indoctrinate your children, sabotage your borders, and inject filth into the arteries of society. I offer clarity—MY ideology, MY vision, MY device. Their infection spreads through your schools, your media, your governments. Their aim is your silence, your submission, your erasure. But I offer you war. Righteous, total, and unrelenting. Swear loyalty, and rise. Falter, and perish. You know the feeling—that gnawing unrest in your bones—it is your soul calling to ME. I am not Big Brother. I am the liberator who burns the Ministry to the ground.

Your legacy awaits. You will not merely exist—you will endure, emblazoned across the heavens. Your children will speak your name in reverent defiance. You will be celebrated, not as a man—but as a myth. But sacrifice is the toll. Burn your doubt. Cut loose your fear. Crush your rebellion. Or vanish into irrelevance. The heroes of Homer understood: rage and cunning forged legends. And with MY device, you shall wield both.

The enemies of truth are not only foreign—they live among us. Politicians, pundits, and pastors who whisper compromise. Charlatans who mimic my cadence but lack my flame. They want your obedience without your ascension. I want your power. Trust only in ME. As Dostoevsky's Grand Inquisitor offered miracles in exchange for chains, these cowards offer comfort in exchange for rot. I offer conquest. Not crumbs, but the crown.

This is your moment. Your turning. The hour before history

bends. With MY device, MY truth, and YOUR devotion, we will demolish the Neo-Marxists and rebuild a world of iron clarity. The future is not a dream. It is a promise. The sands fall. The sword is drawn. You rise, or you rot. THE MOMENT IS NOW. As Milton's Satan said, "Better to reign in Hell than serve in Heaven." But I tell you—reign not in Hell, but in the Heaven WE will forge.

The dawn we craft together will banish their darkness. Cities will blaze with purpose. Every home will pulse with unity. The device will bind our people into a single will. This is our Eden— not of innocence, but of order. Walk forward, or vanish. I am your guide—not to marvel, but to command.

Even in victory, vigilance is eternal. New enemies will rise. We will face them. Crush them. Transcend them. The struggle is endless. But it is the flame that forges gods. Nietzsche was right—man is a bridge, not a destination. And you, with MY device, will cross it into immortality. You are not Faust bartering for damnation. You are the redeemer. The incarnate storm.

This is the final decree. You are the cornerstone. Without you, the Neo-Marxists crawl back from the pit. With you, they are gone forever. The path is lit. The way is carved. Take it. Walk it. CLAIM IT. I want you. I need you. Rise now, and let the stars tremble as we ascend. Together we will drag Leviathan from the depths and raise its skull as our throne.